DANGER IN PARADISE

DANGER IN PARADISE

by

Carol A. Hughes

This book is a work of fiction, Names, characters, places, businesses, organizations, and incidents either are the product of the author's imagination or are used fictitiously. Any resemblance to actual events, locales or persons, living or dead, is entirely coincidental.

With the exception of quotes used in reviews, no part of this book may be reproduced, downloaded, decompiled, reverse engineered, or stored in a retrieval system, or transmitted by any form or by any means, electronic, mechanical, written, audio, visual, photocopying, recording, or otherwise by means or methods currently in use or yet to be developed, without express written permission of the author.

DEDICATION

To C.E.C

CONTENTS

CHAPTER 1

Jake Rafferty swerved the Ferrari around the rear fender of the silver Bentley directly in front of him. "Get outta the bloody way!" he shouted whipping through the early evening traffic sedately gliding along Monaco's *Boulevard Albert 1er*. He could hear the alarms shrieking from more than a block away. Of all days for something to go wrong. Étienne Devereux knew that he had to be in Geneva for the security conference meeting earlier today. So why, of all days, did he decide that today he didn't need security?

Rocketing past the startled face of the tuxedoed Bentley driver, Jake lasered, in on the four-storey white rococo building near the far end of the block that was his destination. "Derrick," he barked bringing his cell phone back to his ear, "get the team over here now! And bring the Rock."

Tossing the phone onto the empty passenger's seat, he barely heard the "10-4" as he jerked the wheel to the right and rocketed across three lanes of oncoming traffic to careen to a stop directly in front of the etched glass lobby doors of the Banque de Monaco building.

Snatching up his cell phone as he threw open the driver's door, Jake unfolded his 6'3" frame from behind the wheel and raced across the sidewalk. Behind him the undulating wail of approaching sirens filled the balmy night air. Grabbing the polished brass lever, he yanked the lobby door open and charged into the building.

"Monsieur Rafferty! It's the Penthouse!" the scarlet and gold uniformed guard called out from behind the mahogany security desk.

Never breaking stride, Jake headed straight for the bank of gleaming elevators at the rear of the plant-filled lobby. "Gerard, release the elevators. They'll be quicker than the stairs." Reaching the elevators, Jake stabbed the darkened control buttons.

"It is no good, *M'sieur.* The fire has broken through to the shaft. I can't override the safety shut down system."

Spinning on the balls of his feet Jake headed for the nearby stairwell. "Who's still upstairs?"

"M'sieur Devereux et les deux femmes."

Shouldering his way into the rear stairwell, Jake took the stairs three at a time as he raced towards the burning fourth floor penthouse suite. He could hear the roar of the raging flames growing louder and louder the higher he climbed. Bloody hell, this was his worst nightmare coming true he thought as he rounded the stairwell's metal hand rail and continued racing higher.

Reaching the fourth floor landing, he quickly ran his hand over the closed metal fire door. And just as quickly snatched it away from the red hot metal. This is not good, he thought, as he grabbed the shoulder of his left jacket sleeve, and with one yank, ripped it free.

Grabbing the top opening with both hands, he quickly ripped the sleeve in two length-wise strips. Swiftly tying one strip around his nose and mouth, he then wrapped the second strip around the palm of his left hand. Squatting down until he was eye level with the lever door handle, he cautiously inched the heavy protective door open and peered into the smoke blacken service corridor running along the back of the penthouse suite.

He was looking into the heart of a fiery inferno. An inferno so intense that it instantly sucked the breath out of him. Definite bloody hell, he thought as he momentarily turned his face away to pull cooler air into his lungs, as waves of heat billowed through the door crack and slammed into him.

The clanging of the fire bells was deafening as he swung the door open wide enough for him to shoulder roll into the roiling soot-laden clouds of smoke and heat billowing along the entire length of the flame-engulfed corridor ceiling. The waves of heat pulsing down from the ceiling were staggering as he rolled to his feet and spun to the right to race the ten yards to the service door leading into the kitchen and pantry area at the rear of the penthouse.

Reaching his target, he was startled to find the door leading directly into the rear storage pantry area ajar. *Breach* his mind screamed as he took in the open door at a glance. At the same instant a nearby section of the flame engulfed corridor ceiling came crashing down from overhead. In a flash he dived into the apartment and slammed the door shut behind him to block out the deadly smoke and flames filling the corridor outside. The deafening cacophony of the clanging of the fire bells was instantly muffled by the closed door. None of the security alarm bells inside the penthouse were going off. Their absence was deafening compared to the din of the hallway.

Where was Devereux? Had they snatched him already?

The only sounds he could hear in the place, outside of the muffled chaos from the corridor, was the loud crackling of flames burning through the walls and ceilings of the surrounding rooms. That, and the explosive crash of glass cabinets shattering, as the fire raged through the antique-filled 32 room penthouse.

Security breach his gut kept screaming in alarm as he instinctively rolled into a defensive stance and his gun cleared the shoulder holster under his left arm. Swinging his weapon in 180 degree arcs, he silently advanced into the brightly lit, smoke-filled restaurant-sized kitchen. From his position in the open pantry door, his eyes quickly swept the entire open gourmet kitchen area. He instantly spotted the small figure of a dark-haired woman sprawled face down on the floor on the opposite side of the room.

Moving on cat-like feet, he darted across the twenty feet separating them. Kneeling beside the woman, he did a visual sweep of the area in front of him. Reaching down with his left hand, he did a quick check for a carotid pulse.

There wasn't one.

Somebody was definitely going to pay for this flashed through his mind as he turned away from the body. Like a coiled panther he sprang to his feet and crossed to the double stainless steel sinks on the far side of the room. As he moved, he pulled off the cloth strip covering his nose and mouth, while keeping a cautious eye on the door leading out into the rest of the apartment. Quickly turning on the cold water faucet he soaked the cloth. Then, using his elbow to shut off the faucet, he rapidly tied the dripping cloth back around his nose and mouth before slipping quickly out of the kitchen and into the apartment itself.

Swiftly and silently he cleared each room he passed as he made his way into the heart of the complex of rooms that comprised the $20 million Devereux penthouse overlooking Monaco's yacht-filled Port Hercules harbor. Where the bloody hell was Derrick and the rest of his backup? It shouldn't be taking them that long to get here.

Drawing closer to the center rooms, the thicker and blacker the smoke was becoming. The growing crackle of the advancing flames devouring the centuries old oil masterpieces adorning many of the walls was the only thing he encountered as he advanced steadily towards the master bedroom suite at the far end of the penthouse.

Using his left hand, Jake pulled out his cell phone and flipped it open without lowering his eyes from the gun sweeping arcs in front of him. Punching in the first speed dial number he raised the phone to his ear as it was picked up on the first ring.

"Jake, where are you?"

"On site. The cook is dead."

"Devereux?"

"I haven't made contact yet." Jake continued pushing through the oily smoke, "we've been breached."

"I'm outside. I'm coming up."

"No! You can't do anything up here."

Suddenly, overhead the weight of the raging inferno caused the rapidly blackening ceiling to groan in protest. Instinctively, Jake picked up his pace.

"Secure the Rock and alert Moreau," he finished over the roar of the surrounding inferno.

Flipping the phone closed, he slipped it back into his trouser pocket. As he did, one end of a flaming roof beam plunged through the ceiling in front of him and speared the center of the burgundy and royal blue Aubusson runner lining the main hallway. At the same, instant fiery sparks peppered his face and head. Quickly brushing the sizzling sparks out of his dark hair, he hurried around the obstacle.

That's when he spotted the form of the second woman crumpled alongside the right wall half way between him and the doors to the master bedroom suite. From the willowy outline he could tell it was the American nurse, Riley Cooper.

Moving towards her, the primitive part of his brain analyzed the chaos surrounding him. Whoever they were, they came in through the back door and took out the cook before she could trigger the alarm. That meant they were pros, he concluded as he quickly closed the distance between him and fallen woman.

Reaching Riley's side, he quickly touched the soft flesh along the side of her neck. Feeling the slow pulse throbbing under his finger tips he was relieved to discover she was still alive. Even if she was completely unresponsive to his touch. A quick glance between the burning roof beam that had set the carpet on fire, and the closed doors of the master suite fifty feet to his right, instantly narrowed his options to only one choice.

"Looks like it's your lucky day, princess," he muttered as he quickly slipped his gun back into its holster under his left arm. Grabbing Riley under her arms, he hefted her up over his left shoulder. Rising to his feet, he hurried on towards the master suite.

Ignoring the awkwardness of having an unconscious woman draped over his shoulder, Jake quickly reached the double doors to the suite. Brushing the curved teak doors with the back of his hand confirmed they were not hot. Reaching around his passenger's legs and pulling his out 9mm, Jake silently eased open the door to the master suite.

Slipping inside, he closed the door behind him to keep out the deadly smoke and flames. Doing a quick visual scan of the room, Jake took in the two-room, book-lined suite that served as Étienne Devereux's private bedroom and lounge area. He had always liked the clean masculine lines of both the room and its furniture.

The room was in semi-darkness and hushed.

Jake's eyes were instantly drawn to the bright blade of light from the crack of the open bathroom door that knifed across the king sized master bed and the still form of Étienne Devereux. Clad in ivory-colored silk pajamas, Devereux laid motionless under the deep purple silk spread covering the vast expanse of his bed that dominated the suite.

Flames from a small wood fire in the black marble fireplace at the foot of the bed danced merrily behind the glass fire screen. The only sound in the room was the soft ticking of the 18th century silver and gold rococo Telleruhr clock on the mantle.

Jake swiftly crossed to his client and, for a third time in as many minutes, checked for a pulse.

Finding none, he straightened up and shifted Riley's weight to keep her from sliding off his shoulder. Damnit. This shouldn't have happened. Looking down at his dead client Jake shook his head in frustration.

A booming crash reverberated suddenly along the blazing corridor outside.

In a flash, Jake dumped the unconscious Riley on the bed at Devereux's feet, and shot across the room to the door. He eased it open an eye's width and peered into the burning corridor leading to the front of the penthouse. Through the mayhem of the roiling black smoke and dancing flames engulfing the entire corridor he spotted a phalanx of red-suited and masked firefighters battling their way towards him.

About bloody time, he thought as he threw a quick glance over his shoulder to the two silent figures on the nearby bed.

CAROL A. HUGHES

CHAPTER 2

Breathing was the most painful thing Riley Cooper had ever done in her entire life. Not even getting kicked by that wild mustang when she was twelve and dislocating her shoulder had hurt anywhere near as much as breathing was hurting her right now.

Maybe if she just kept her eyes closed that would make it easier to breathe. Riley knew she was floating on a cloud – well, she was pretty sure it was a cloud since it was so soft and comfortable. Was she dead? Can you think when you're dead she wondered? Does being dead hurt this much? She couldn't be dead! She still hasn't finished with that thieving sidewinder Mark yet. Or, had she? She couldn't remember. It hurt too much – to breathe.

As much as she didn't want to do it, she was just going to have to open her eyes to find out if she was dead or not. Reluctantly, she finally managed to open them just a crack.

Big mistake.

The bright light stabbed straight into her brain.

Her first thought - once she could breathe through this new wave of pain – I don't think I'm dead. It hurt almost as much as breathing.

Maybe she should just keep her eyes closed. The dark was nice. It felt warm with trickles of cool running through it. That was nice. She wondered how it would feel to just float away on that trickle of warm and cool and dark.

So she did.

~~~

The BEEP …BEEP …BEEP of the heart monitor pulled Riley back to shore.

She had to check on her patient.

Why was he on a heart monitor? He didn't need a heart monitor for his back injury. Did something happen on the last shift? Bill Larson hadn't said anything in Report. That wasn't like him. She needed to find out right now.

~~~

"Welcome back," the shadowy figure in the corner of the room shifted slightly in the visitor's chair as a confused Riley looked around the equipment cluttered hospital room.

"What am I doing in a hospital?" She focused all of her attention on the visitor who was partially obscured by the array of monitoring equipment surrounding her hospital bed.

Her bed? Not Mr. Devereux's. She pulled herself up into a sitting position so she could see around the equipment. "What happened?" Her voice was as rough as scraped cowhide.

As she sat up, her mysterious visitor stood so she was finally able to see who it was. The British guy who was the head of Mr. Devereux's private security people. The one with the lower lip that she wanted to nibble every time she saw it. - That is, if she hadn't permanently sworn off of all good looking men, thanks to her ex.

"Mr. Rafferty? What are you doing here?" Riley shot a quick glance around the room just to confirm that she really was in the hospital, and not having a weird dream. "What happened? Was I in an accident?"

He shook his head at her. "No. It was the penthouse."

Crossing to the side of her bed Jake couldn't help noticing the fine bone structure underlying her heart-shaped face. With all of the IVs they had been pumping into her to clean out her system he was surprised she hadn't bloated up like a water-filled balloon. Her short, tousled chestnut hair may give her a slightly sultry, sexy look. But the fire in chocolate brown eyes was flashing enough heat at him to immediately dampen his surprising physical reaction to her.

And what is going on with this sudden surge in his libido? He had watched her many times on the Penthouse's security monitors and had never noticed anything personal about her except for the fact that she appeared to be a highly competent private duty nurse. And he should know since the Devereuxes had gone through 19 of them in the 16 months he and his team had been handling their security.

But she wasn't Étienne Devereux's nurse right now. What she was, was the sole survivor of an arson fire that killed two people. - One of them being his billionaire client.

And *Executive Security*'s reputation was on the line thanks to Devereux's death. So he had way too much riding on finding out exactly what went wrong in that penthouse to let his libido get in the way.

"What happened at the penthouse?" she interrupted his musing.

"Why don't you tell me?"

"Tell you? I wouldn't be asking you what happened if I knew," she snapped at him. "Now, would I?"

At that moment the door to her room swung open and a broad shouldered man with thoughtful eyes walked in. He was followed by a thin, dark-haired man in a white lab coat who towered over him by a good six inches.

Glancing over at the two men as they approached the foot of Riley's bed, Jake nodded slightly to the shorter man. "*Inspecteur.*"

Returning Jake's nod with one of his own the man locked eyes with Riley. "*Mademoiselle,* how are you feeling?" he asked her in a soft voice.

His voice may be non-threatening, but Riley instantly sensed a timbre of iron-willed determination underlying the softness. And although he was looking at her with a neutral expression on his face she didn't miss the predatory glint lurking beneath the surface of his gray eyes.

"I've had better days," she answered as she straightened her spine in order not to appear helpless to this stranger. "Who are you, please?"

The white-coated man stepped forward before his companion could reply. "I'm your doctor, *M'seille.* I'm Julien Fournier. I've been treating you for severe smoke inhalation since you were brought in."

Riley turned her attention to the doctor. "How long have I been here?"

"Since yesterday evening."

"24 hours?"

"27 actually," Fournier replied.

She returned her attention to the other man who had been silently observing her the whole time. "Are you with the police?"

"Yes."

When he didn't continue, Jake stepped closer to Riley's bed and made the introductions. "Miss Cooper, this is Chief *Inspecteur* Marcel Moreau of the Nice Police Department. He's assigned to the *Sûreté Publique.*"

"Nice, France?" she gave Jake a puzzled look. "How did I end up in France?"

"You're not in France, *M'seille*," Moreau indicated the room around them. "You're in Monaco's *Centre Hospitalier Princesse Grace*."

"Since Monaco is such a small territory, with so little crime, France provides police support for the Principality," Jake explained.

Riley nodded in response, then focused her attention on the Frenchman. "Then you can tell me what happened."

Moreau turned his head slightly towards Jake and raised his eyebrows in silent question. To which Jake gave him a half shrug in reply.

"Excuse me," Riley interrupted their muted exchange. "I'm over here. And I'm the one who asked the question."

Moreau turned his attention back to her with a slight bemused half smile on his face at the impatience in her voice. "*Mais oui*. I just assumed that *M'sieur* Rafferty had already filled you in on the details of the tragedy."

Jake saw Riley pale slightly and grip the rails of her hospital bed with her right hand until her knuckles turned white. At the same time she shot him a cold, accusatory look before quickly turning her attention back to the policeman. "What tragedy?" she asked brusquely. "Who else was injured and how badly?"

"You don't know?" Moreau asked her in a low-keyed voice.

"Of course I don't," she said glaring at him. "I just woke up right before you walked in." She threw a look over at Jake standing silently to her left. Turning back to Moreau and her doctor standing at his side, she continued. "Since Doctor Fournier has been treating me for smoke inhalation, I can figure out for myself that there was a fire. How bad was it? Are *M'sieur* Devereux and Carmela OK?"

13

"Unfortunately, no." Moreau answered with a slight shake of his head.

Riley felt an iron vise clamp around her heart. "Are they still alive?"

The silence in the room answered the question for her.

"How?" Against her will tears filled her eyes. Looking over at Jake's grim face she continued to him. "Why didn't security get them out in time?"

Jake crossed his arms in front of his chest before responding. "My people weren't there."

"What?" disbelief shot through Riley. "They're always there."

"Not last night."

"Why in the world, not?"

"Devereux insisted that the whole team accompany his wife to the charity event at the Palace."

"Why? Who in the world is going to mug her at the Royal Palace?"

"She was wearing her necklace."

"The fancy diamond one?"

Jake nodded in response.

"And I'll bet so were a lot of the other women at the event." Riley scowled at him. "In case you haven't noticed, diamonds are quite common around here."

"Not a $157 million one like the Constanza Diamond," Moreau points out.

Riley's eyes widen in shock as she looked over at the Frenchman. "$157 …. MILLION. Are you serious?"

It's Moreau's turn to nod in response.

"But it's just a rock," she said shaking her head at him. How in the world could one sparkly rock be worth more than all of the Lazy H's 200,000 acres and its entire 50,000 head of prime Wyoming beef?

Riley glanced over at Jake Rafferty and caught him silently watching her.

No wonder the Devereuxes had a permanent team of security personnel with them at all time. But then again, she thought wryly, when you're a billionaire international banker like Étienne Devereux was – 'had been' – she mentally corrected herself. It made sense you'd want the best security that money could buy. Especially if your high maintenance wife was floating around the international playground of the rich and famous decked out in a $157 million bauble.

"Obviously, a very rare one," Dr. Fournier's comment snapped her attention back to the three men ringing her hospital bed.

Riley glanced back and forth between the Jake and Moreau. "The fire was an accident. Wasn't it?"

Neither man attempted to answer her question.

"How did it start? I never smelled any smoke or heard any alarms going off."

Jake's right eyebrow arched at her in disbelief.

Riley caught that and clenched her jaw as anger flashed across her face like a summer squall racing across a small lake. "I'm telling you that I didn't hear or smell anything."

She turned back to Moreau. "Where did the fire start?"

"We think in the medical room. The arson investigation isn't fully completed yet. But so far they've found twelve origination points spread throughout the apartment."

"Twelve?"

Jake watched the anger flee as her face filled with stunned disbelief. Was it real, or was she just that good of an actress, he wondered as Riley shook her head as if to make the news disappear.

"That doesn't make any sense," she said as she tried to puzzle out the sequence of events. "How could anyone get into the place with all of the security there is." She looked back over at Jake. "Even if the security team wasn't there. There are all kinds of electronic locks and backup systems that control who can come into the residence."

She turned back to Moreau as she continued. "Once you go out, it's harder to get back in than getting into Fort Knox." This time she shook her head at the Frenchman. "Are you telling me that Carmela let somebody in after the security team left with *Madame* Devereux?"

"What makes you think it was Carmela?" Moreau asked.

"It was Bill Larson's day off. That's why I was working the night shift."

Moreau interrupted her. "How long is your shift?"

"Twelve hours on, twelve off."

Satisfied with her answer, Moreau nodded at her to continue.

"So that left Carmela Paulino, the cook, and me on duty for the evening. *M'sieur* Devereux was planning on retiring early because it was his physical therapy day." She glanced over at Moreau to make sure he was following her. "He crushed two discs in his back falling off his polo pony during a match last year. So he's always in a lot of pain. Especially on the days when he does physical therapy. On those days he has an injection for pain and usually retires early to read or watch TV."

Moreau shot Jake a quick look, that Riley missed. "The back door was standing open when *M'sieur* Rafferty arrived on the scene," Moreau told her.

Riley's eyes narrowed as she turned to Jake. "Why would Carmela leave the door open?"

"What makes you think Carmela left the door open?" Jack said.

"Well I didn't. So who else could do it?"

"What about *M'sieur* Devereux?" Moreau asked.

She shook her head at him. "Definitely not. I seriously doubt if that man even knew where the kitchen was located. Much less the rear door to the place." She continued shaking her head at Moreau, "With all of his money Mr. Devereux was terrified of being kidnapped for ransom." She jerked her head towards Jake "That's why he was surrounded by an armed security team 24/7."

Riley turned her full attention to Jake. "Didn't your people think it was strange that he wouldn't have at least one security person there given how afraid he was of kidnappers targeting him?"

Jake shook his head at her. "The team leader confirmed it personally with Devereux. He thought the same thing. But Devereux insisted that he wanted the entire security team with his wife since she was being escorted to the dinner by one of his most important clients. And the two of them were personally hosting the guest of honor."

He turned to Moreau. "So they weren't just guarding the necklace."

The *Inspecteur* looked at him. "They weren't guarding the necklace to begin with."

"What do you mean?" Jake said. "That's part of their job."

17

Moreau responded with a slight shake of his head. "*Non*, not that night."

"Why not that night?"

"Because she wasn't wearing it," Riley interrupted.

As both men looked in her direction, she continued as she locked eyes with Moreau. "She wore a fake copy."

"And you know this because why?"

"I don't. I'm just guessing since you said it wasn't part of the security team's job that night. And I understand a lot of folks with expensive jewelry have fake copies made for security reasons."

She turned back to Jake. "So that means that Mr. Devereux must have wanted to impress his two guests by having the entire security team escort them to the Palace dinner that night. Even though his wife wasn't wearing her real diamonds."

Glaring over at the Frenchman Jake's eyes and voice were flinty. "Is this true that she was wearing the paste copy?"

Moreau nodded "yes."

"Who told you?"

"*Madame* Devereux when we opened the safe in the penthouse and found it empty."

"Who was with *Madame* Devereux that they needed the entire security team guarding them?" Riley asked.

Jake finally broke off eye contact with the Frenchman and gave her a half shrug. "A Russian oil billionaire named Alexei Zhukov and the Afghani Minister of Education and Health, Aziz Sayed Hamidi."

"The charity dinner was to raise money for schools and hospitals in Afghanistan, if I remember correctly," Moreau explained. "*Madame* Devereux presented the Minister with a personal check of $15 million Euros at the dinner."

Jake wasn't surprised by that statement. He had known Marcel Moreau since first arriving in Monaco more than ten years ago from London. Moreau always liked to play it close to the vest. But Jake knew from personal experience that if a flea farted anywhere in Monaco, Moreau would know all about before the flea did.

"That sounds like her," Riley nodded. "She's always busy with her charity work."

Noticing the smudges of exhaustion under Riley's eyes, Dr. Fournier suddenly interrupted them by moving to the side of Riley's bed. Using the side mounted control panel, he raised the head of her bed so that she could lean back and rest as he glanced over at the two men. "That is enough for now, gentlemen. My patient is still recovering and needs to rest."

A look of relief filled Riley's pale face as she took advantage of his gesture to lean back against the upraised bed. She really was exhausted – more than she realized until just now. "Thank you, Doctor," she said as Fournier helped her find a comfort position in bed. "You're right. I am tired." She closed her eyes as she murmured, "very tired."

Jake caught the decisive look that filled Moreau's eyes. But before he could even wonder what was going through his mind, the *Inspecteur* turned to the doctor.

"Is *M'seille* Cooper in any immediate danger, health-wise?" Moreau asked.

Fournier took in the grayish pallor of exhaustion and the dark circles under Riley's eyes. Lifting her right wrist, he checked her pulse. It was weaker than he would like, but steady. Gently placing her arm back on the bed, he turned to answer Moreau's question.

"No. She'll make a full recovery. But right now she needs to rest."

"Good." Moreau said nodding his head once. Then he looked Fournier in the eye and dropped his bombshell.

"We'll see to it that she gets a lot of rest in jail."

"Jail!" Riley's eyes sprang open and she jerked upright to stare at Moreau in confusion. At her side Fournier's face filled with shocked disbelief. Only Jake seemed totally unsurprised by Moreau's statement.

"What are you talking about?" she demanded as disbelief tinged her voice. "I didn't have anything to do with what happened."

"Really?" Moreau said in a maddeningly neutral voice. "Then how do you explain the fact that your fingerprints are the only ones on the empty alcohol bottles which were used throughout the apartment to start the fire that killed Étienne Devereux and Carmela Paulino?"

Before she could open her mouth to defend herself, there was a quick knock on the door. Pushing it open, two male and a lone female uniformed police officers shouldered their way into the already crowded room.

"*M'seille* Riley Cooper," Moreau intoned in a solemn voice as his three officers lined up behind him. "I am arresting you on suspicion of arson, murder and burglary."

CHAPTER 3

"Seventeen hours!" Riley slowly swung her drooping head back and forth in equal parts exasperation and exhaustion. "And I keep telling you the same thing over and over again." The smudges under her eyes had turned to purplish bruises of utter exhaustion. "I didn't kill anybody and I don't know anything.

The half-filled paper cup of cold coffee sitting on the wooden table in front of her had formed a milky skim across its surface hours ago. Somehow a fly had gotten trapped in the closed room with them. Now it was floating silently in the middle of the cup. Slowly lifting her eyes from the tiny corpse she returned Moreau's silent stare as she let out a long, weary breath.

Bless Dr. Fournier for refusing to allow Moreau to take her out of the hospital in her patient's nightgown. If he had, she'd be at more of a psychological disadvantage than she already was. The *Inspecteur* hadn't been happy about the delay when Fournier had insisted that Moreau's department had to provide her with a set of civilian clothing for the trip to the police station.

It had taken close to an hour for his female officer to make the trip and return with a new pair of pencil-leg jeans, a billowy white silk blouse and an oversized, cream-yellow cashmere sweater to ward off the chill of any air conditioner. Upon seeing the clothes, Riley's first thought was that while the woman had a crappy job, at least she had great taste in clothes.

She had to admit to herself that she hadn't anticipated silk and cashmere. But then again this was Monaco so what did she honestly expect? Definitely not Jake Rafferty's reminding the policewoman to include a set of underwear in her purchases. Preferably silk and lace, he had said as the woman hurried away under Moreau's less than amused glare.

She was still wondering if he did that out of consideration for her. Or was he just amusing himself at her expense? But Jake Rafferty was not her problem at the moment. Instead, a very suspicious police inspector was. So she returned her attention to the man in question and said, "I'm a nurse. Of course my fingerprints would be on the bottles. We used the alcohol to sterilize the injection area when we gave Mr. Devereux his shots."

She continued looking across the scarred and gouged table at Moreau and the middle-aged female police stenographer sitting to his left. "And I'm still waiting to speak to someone from the American Embassy."

"Of course," Moreau dipped his chin at her. "Just as soon as they arrive. Until then, shall we continue?"

She felt like the tail end of a nine week cattle drive. And probably smelled like one too, she thought blinking to get the grit of exhaustion out of her blood shot eyes. Letting out another long breath of frustration she straightened up and arched her weary spine in order to force some fresh blood into her aching back and cramping muscles.

"No. Enough is enough," she could feel a tiny spark of anger suddenly flicker to life. How could anyone think she would do anything to endanger or harm one of her patients? "I almost died in that fire. My two friends did."

She glared across the table at him. "If I knew anything, anything at all, that could possibly help you. I would tell you. But I don't. And that isn't going to change no matter how many times you ask me to tell you what happened." The anger growing inside her gave renewed strength to her voice as she continued to glare across the table at Moreau. "I can't tell you what I don't know."

What was wrong with him? If it hadn't been for Jake Rafferty arriving when he did, she would have died along with the others.

"The last thing I remember from Wednesday is getting into the shower to get ready for work."

Moreau ignored her last comment. "'Friends'?" he said in his maddeningly calm voice. "That's a strange word to use for an employer. Especially one as wealthy as *M'sieur* Devereux."

So what if he was her employer? He was a nice, kind man. At least he had been to her. And, on top of that, he had made her feel at home – even if it was his home and not hers.

"Have you talked to Bill Larson?" Maybe he knows something that can help you."

"Such as what?"

"I don't know. I'm just trying to be helpful."

Moreau leaned forward slightly in his chair to better see the notes he had scribbled on the small, spiral-bound notepad laying on the table in front of him. From her position across from him Riley could see that the page was filled with handwriting that had been done with a leaky black ball point pen. From where she sat she couldn't tell if the writing was in English or French. To her it just looked like upside down chicken scratchings.

"*M'sieur* Larson had the evening off. He left several hours before the fire began and did not return to the residence until 8:00 am the next morning."

"What time did he leave?"

Moreau looked across at her. "You don't know?"

She shook her head at him. "I didn't see him leave." A small furrow appeared between her eyebrows. "At least I don't remember seeing him leave."

Had she even see him at all on Wednesday? Why couldn't she remember anything? She never had this problem before.

"You're lack of memory is very convenient, *non*?

Anger flashed in Riley's eyes. "No, it is not 'convenient' at all. Two people that I liked very much died a horrible death. I was there and I can't remember a single thing about what happened that caused it." Shaking her head in frustration at him, she continued. "So 'no,' Inspector. It most definitely is not convenient at all."

"The Constanza," Moreau said. "You admired it."

"Which one?" she snapped, frustrated by his refusal to stop wasting time badgering her instead of focusing on finding the real killer. "*Madame* or her diamond?"

Moreau smiled at her sudden flare of temper. "$157 million is a bit more than what your ranch is worth. You may no longer have your ranch. But that much money would certainly make life easy again for you, *n'est pas*? No more working for other people. People like the Devereuxes."

Fear flooded through her. "The Lazy H? How do you know that?"

Moreau's smile had as much warmth as a cobra's. "I'm a policeman. It's my job to know about things like you losing your family's ranch to your ex-husband in a divorce."

"I didn't 'lose' it. It was stolen."

Moreau gives her a small Gallic shrug. "It was in your family for a long time, *non*?"

"Five generations," she said as anger started to dissolve away the exhaustion. "But what do my divorce, and my private business, have to do with what happened at the penthouse?"

Understanding suddenly broadsided her. "Oh, no!" she violently shook her head at him. "You don't honestly think I killed them just so I could steal another woman's necklace because my thieving ex-husband stole from me?"

Moreau ignored her outburst as he stole a quick glance at his notes then glanced back up at her with a knowing look in his eyes.

"The money from the sale of the missing necklace would go a long way towards fighting your ex-husband to regain your lost land."

The gray-haired stenographer next to Moreau was perched on the edge of her chair with her fingers poised over the keys of her steno machine as Riley continued shaking her head at Moreau in denial. "That's insane."

"Is it? $157 million is a lot of money. People have killed for far less."

"Not me." Riley snapped back, wanting to reach across the table and smack that knowing look off his face. As that thought flashed across her mind, she realized that her temper was going to make her look guiltier than the Frenchman already thought she was if she doesn't step on it real quick.

Taking a deep breath and slowly sitting back in her chair she looked Moreau straight in the eye. "I'm a nurse. My job is to take care of my patients. Not harm them."

Moreau rested his right hand atop the small note pad lying in front of him on the table as he regarded her with a steady gaze. "I don't think you pulled this heist off by yourself."

"I didn't pull off any 'heist,' Inspector. I'm as much a victim as the others."

He dipped his head slightly towards her. "That I believe."

"You do?" Relief flooded through her. Finally, they were getting somewhere. "Then why…?"

"I believe," he cut her off, "that you were betrayed by whomever you were working with."

"Working with!" Riley jumped to her feet in angry disbelief. "I wasn't working with anyone!"

Moreau gave her another laconic Gallic shrug as he grandly swept his hand towards the chair behind her. "Please, *M'seille*. There is no need to shout just because you are upset."

"Upset? You don't know the half of it," Riley said glaring at him. She yanked her chair closer and sat back down. "You're accusing me of being a thief and a murderer. What do you expect me to be?"

"Smarter than you have been so far."

Riley clenched her teeth together to keep from making a retort she just might regret. As she did, the Inspector settled back into his wooden chair and met her angry glare with his own, which was totally dispassionate. "I don't believe that you expected to be trapped in the burning apartment along with the others."

Riley opened her mouth to protest, but Moreau held up two fingers to stop her as he continued in a low voice. "Whoever set those fires and stole the necklace murdered Étienne Devereux and Madame Paulino. That is a fact we both can agree on, *non?*

Riley gave him a sullen nod of agreement. "Yes."

Moreau returned her nod with one of his own as a look of satisfaction filled his face. "And whoever did this is going to go to prison for a very long time."

It was Riley's turn to give him a shrug in silent response.

"You yourself pointed out how difficult it was to enter the apartment due to all of the security measures."

Riley regarded him warily as he continued.

"You had access to the penthouse. Your fingerprints are the only ones found on the bottles of alcohol used to start the fires throughout the penthouse."

Riley strained forward and opened her mouth to defend herself, but Moreau cut off her protests by holding up his forefinger to silence her as he pressed on. "You had access to the safe in the penthouse."

"No!" Riley shook her head decisively at him. "I didn't even know there was a safe in the place."

"With all of the jewels Madame Devereux owned?" Moreau said in disbelief. "Do you honestly expect me, or anyone, to believe that you did not know that the Devereuxes had a safe in their home for their valuables?"

Riley leaned forward and locked eyes with him. "I never gave it a thought since I just assumed that they kept all of their valuables downstairs in the bank. After all, he owned the bank along with the building."

As Riley eased back in her battered wooden chair Moreau cupped his right hand and flicked his fingers upward in dismissal. "No matter. That doesn't change the facts – or the evidence. You were inside the Penthouse when the fires broke off. You had access to all of the alarms that had been shut off. Your prints were found on the empty alcohol bottles."

It was Moreau's turn to lock eyes with Riley. "You are the one being accused here with the arson-robbery murder of two people." He paused momentarily to watch the effect his words were having on her. "Based upon the evidence I have no choice but to charge you with murder, *M'seille.*"

As his words echoed through her mind, Riley hissed out a sharp breath of disbelief. This couldn't be happening to her. She had never deliberately hurt a single person in her whole life. How could anyone even begin to believe that she would deliberately cause two people to die such a horrible death?

Riley fisted her left hand and gripped it tightly with her right as she ignored Moreau's stare. She inhaled deeply to steady her nerves and lasso her fear. Growing up, her father had taught her how to do three things really well. Ride a horse. Shoot a gun. And play poker.

And the first rule of any good poker player was to know when to put on your "poker face". Especially if you're holding a losing hand. As far as she was concerned, sitting in a French jail, even if it was located in Monaco, accused of killing two people just to steal a piece of over-priced jewelry, definitely ranked as a losing hand in her book any day of the week.

In fact, it ranked right along side of her getting taken for a fool by her conniving ex-husband and his equally evil and greedy father. Even now she couldn't understand why she had been so surprised when she found out that truth about him. After all, the apple never falls far from the tree.

But Mark Scanlon and her ex-father-in-law weren't her problem at the moment. *Inspecteur* Marcel Moreau was. And from the looks of things she was in a whole lot more trouble than the time she encountered that rampaging grizzly bear attacking her dog Winston.

"I am going to repeat what I have been telling you from the beginning," Riley said in a voice as stiff as an iron fence post. "I had absolutely nothing to do with the deaths of either Étienne Devereux or Carmela Paulino.

"The last thing I can clearly remember is getting into the shower on Wednesday afternoon to get ready for work," she continued. "And the very next thing I remember was waking up in the hospital room and being told that there had been a fatal fire and a robbery."

"What about the other fire?"

"What other fire?"

Moreau made a show of once again consulting his notes on the table as she tried to figure out what he's talking about. "There wasn't any other fire at the penthouse since I've been there."

Moreau looked up from his notes and gave a small shake of his head as he slowly sat back in his battered chair and steepled his fingers under his chin. "The one you set to your husband's truck."

Dread twisted Riley's guts into a giant knot as she inhaled sharply and her eyes widen in disbelief. "How did you . . .?" she whispered, momentarily stunned by this unexpected turn. "There were no charges filed."

Moreau's face may have been dead-panned, but his eyes gave away his satisfaction. Belying his victory with a non-committal half shrug of his right shoulder Moreau pointed to his notebook with a forefinger. "No. But there was a police report made." He looked over at her ashen face, "Your husband demanded that you be arrested. But the Sheriff decided not to press charges against you for trespassing and vandalism.

"Why was that? I have to wonder," Moreau added.

Riley surprised him with her quick recovery. Clenching her jaws and glaring back at him she raised her head in defiance. "He was my "about-to-be ex". So legally the land – and the truck – still belonged to me. It was my father's truck and hell was going to freeze over before I let my conniving about-to-be ex-husband, or anybody else, drive it. Especially since Mark and his father had already stolen my father's land."

"So you blew it up using," Moreau paused momentarily to pretend to consult his notes, "a double barrel shotgun."

It's her turn to shrug back at him. Two could play his game, she decided.

"The fire was an accident. I was shooting out the engine and the tires when the gas tank exploded."

"Clearly the Sheriff must have liked you to have overlooked arresting you."

She gave him a cool look. "He was an old friend of my Dad's. And he knew who the real criminals were that night."

"But, alas," Moreau said placing both forearms on the table in front of him and leaning toward her as he rolled a pen back and forth between his thumbs and forefingers. "Unlike your old family friend, I am not so lucky as to know who the 'real criminal' is in this case."

He paused for effect. "Except for you, of course."

Instead of backing away from him as he expected her to do, she leaned toward him across the table and met his gaze with steely determination in her eyes. "Neither do I, 'Inspecteur'. The only thing I do know, despite what you may think, is that it is not me."

A sharp knock on the door shattered the razor-edged tension in the room. Both Riley and Moreau whipped their heads towards the door as it suddenly swung open to reveal a petite brunette beauty in a blood-red tailored power suit, radiating confidence and simmering anger.

CHAPTER 4

"*Inspecteur* Moreau, why do you always insist on doing this?" the intruder demanded striding into the room like a mini-whirlwind.

Ignoring the pinched look on Moreau's face, the woman set the black leather shoulder briefcase she was carrying on the end of the table and nodded across the table to Riley. "I'm Dominique Roux. You must be Riley."

Before Riley can finish nodding in response Dominique turned her attention back to the silent Moreau. "You know how much I love coming and taking my innocent clients away from you," she said in a friendly mocking tone.

"Client?" Riley said as Moreau arched his eyebrows at the woman.

"Innocent?"

"Yes 'innocent', Marcel," she said as if talking to a slow student.

"Her fingerprints were found all over the alcohol bottles used to fuel the fire." Moreau dropped his chin as he looked up at her standing at the end of the table with both her hands casually resting atop her leather briefcase. "A fire that killed two people."

"And almost killed her," Dominique says with a dismissive wave of her right hand. Glancing down at her case she snapped it open. Pulling out a document she handed it to Moreau.

Riley caught the slight frown that wrinkled Moreau's forehead as he began to read the paperwork in his hand.

As he did, Dominique turned to Riley. "Luckily for you the Judge found it as interesting as I did that your fingerprints were the only ones on any of the alcohol bottles."

Riley shrugged at her. "Why? I'm sure I must have handled them at some time or another."

"How many nurses are on staff?"

"We have one per shift. Two per day. In all, there were a total of eight nurses on staff." Riley caught the encouraging twinkle in Dominique's eyes. At the same instant her mind clicked into action. "Wait a minute. With that many people, there should have been more fingerprints on those bottles than just mine!

Riley shook her head at the now grinning Dominique. "Why didn't I realize that before?"

"Maybe, because you've been a little distracted?" Dominique told her. She then turned her attention back to Moreau, just as he finished reading over the second page of the document she had handed him.

Glancing up at the both of them he laid the document down on the table in front of him. Then he locked eyes with Dominique. "Someone inside the Penthouse disarmed the security systems."

He paused long enough to glance over at Riley before returning his attention to the lawyer. "There were only three people in the residence who could have done that. Two of them are dead."

Dominique gave him a satisfied nod in agreement as she reached into her open briefcase and pulled out a second document. She then proceeded to wave in her right hand to emphasize her point as she spoke. "That's true. But it wasn't my client and I can prove it."

"How?" Riley exclaimed in surprise. "I can't remember anything that happened that evening."

From the look on his face, it was clear Moreau was as curious as Riley to hear Dominique's answer.

"Of course you can't remember. You weren't supposed to."

Glancing back to Moreau, Dominique grinned at him as she held up the document in her hand. "And she doesn't need to remember."

Moreau arched a quizzical eyebrow at her.

"Because this proves that she could not have, and did not, set either the fires, or disarm the alarms," a very satisfied Dominique announced.

Moreau gestured impatiently for her to reveal whatever it was in that report that was putting that Cheshire cat grin on her face. But that only served to widen her grin.

"What is it?" Riley asked jumping into the momentary silence.

Still grinning Dominique looked across the table at her. "The hospital's lab report on your blood work."

"What did they find?"

Dominique's smile widened even further. "Rohypnol."

"Rohypnol! The date rape drug? That's impossible! How?"

Moreau finally broke his stubborn silence. "That doesn't mean anything. She's a nurse. She could have easily injected herself with it."

"I didn't!" Riley snapped as she glared across the table at him. "And why in the world would I? Especially since I almost died in that fire."

She clenched both her jaw and her fists as she continued to glare at him. "Do I look suicidal to you?"

Dominique cocked her eyebrow in admiration at Riley simmering angrily on her side of the table.

But Moreau was unmoved by her anger. "You could have easily have disarmed the security system and then injected yourself with a small dose in order to create an alibi for yourself."

"Are you crazy? What kind of an alibi would that create?"

Moreau calmly returned her angry stare. Then he continued in his low-keyed voice as if she had not interrupted him. "If you were given a polygraph test, you could honestly say that you did not know when the intruders entered, or how many there were. Because you would have been unconscious by then."

He nodded to himself as he glanced over at Riley still glaring at him from across the table. "Of course that would only work if you timed it just right."

Riley opened her mouth to protest but he cut her off before she could utter her first word. "But of course, you would have timed it right, since you are a nurse. And nurses do know these things."

"Intruders," Dominique triumphantly cut him off before Riley could respond. "Then you do know that there was someone else involved."

Moreau swung his glance over to the lawyer. "At this point, we don't know anything since your client is proving to be very uncooperative."

Once again Riley opened her mouth to angrily protest his comment. But she was silenced by a swift hand slash from Dominique who faced off against Moreau with a steely expression on her face.

She slid the lab report across the table towards him. "It's hardly being 'uncooperative' because you can't answer questions about events that occurred while you're unconscious."

Dominique indicated the report that Moreau picked up and began to read. "As you can see, the doctors have confirmed that my client had been unconscious for at least 2 to 3 hours before the fires started." Both she and Riley caught Moreau's look of skepticism when he momentarily glanced up from the report.

Dominique nodded at the report he was holding. "They're basing that conclusion on the amount of the drug that was still in her system two hours after she was admitted to the hospital. Depending upon the victim's weight, they can determine how long it takes for the Rohypnol to be metabolized by the body."

Dominique took a step back from the table and crossed her arms under her breasts. Then she cocked an eyebrow at Moreau who ignored her as he finished reading through the rest of the report. As the silence stretched out between them, Riley glanced anxiously back and forth between the two of them before her eyes finally settled on Dominique's face.

"Then that proves that I didn't have anything to do with what happened."

"Not exactly," Moreau answered without looking up from the report in his hand as Riley whipped her head around towards him.

"But it does prove that you currently do not have enough evidence to charge her with the crime," Dominique shot back at him

Glancing over to Riley and giving her a quick wink Dominique said to her, "or to hold you in custody."

"So I'm free?"

"On bail. For now."

Riley let out a sigh of relief as she nodded her head in understanding. "OK. How much is the bail? And how do I pay it?"

"It's a million Euros."

"A million!"

Moreau's head finally shot up from the report as he watched Riley's face flashed from delight to despair in the blink of an eye.

"I don't have that kind of money."

"That's not a problem," Dominique tells her as she steps to the table and pulls a third document out of her briefcase for Moreau.

"Her bail order," she said as she slid the stapled pages towards Moreau. He made no attempt to pick them up as she straightened up and snapped her briefcase closed.

Turning to Riley, Dominique tells her. "It's already been taken care of." Slipping the case's strap over her shoulder she signals for Riley to follow her out the door.

Instead of moving, Riley glances over at Moreau who is staring silently at Dominique.

"Let's go, your ride is waiting," Dominique says with an impatient edge to her voice.

Moreau finally glances over at Riley. "Don't leave Monaco. I still have more questions for you."

Dominique dips her right shoulder and leans slightly forward to catch Moreau's eyes. "She'll be available. As long as you provide us with proper notice."

Moreau is still looking at Riley as she stands up and pushes her chair back. "Where will you be staying and how do we get in touch with you?"

"You can contact her through my office." Dominique turned towards the door and called over her shoulder to Riley. "Are you coming?"

Riley practically flew across the space separating her from Dominique. "Yes. Of course."

As Dominique stepped through the open door to the busy corridor beyond, Riley paused momentarily to glance over at Moreau. "I know what you think. But I'm telling you the truth. I had absolutely nothing to do with either the robbery or the fire."

With that, Riley turned and hurried out the door in the wake of her attorney.

CAROL A. HUGHES

CHAPTER 5

Focused on getting as far away from the police station as quickly as possible, Riley plowed directly into Dominique when she stepped through the front lobby doors of the police station and came to an abrupt halt.

"Oh, sorry."

Busy grinning at the man casually leaning against a scarlet *Italia* two-seater Ferrari parked directly in front of the station, Dominique waved off her apology.

"Am I good?" Dominique said to Jake Rafferty as she marched over to him. Reaching his side she paused to make a grand sweeping gesture with her arm towards Riley who stood looking at the two of them with a confused expression on her face. "Or am I good?"

Still grinning, Dominique looked over at Riley as she slowly approached. "Lucky for you Jake here was smart enough to get his hands on that lab report. Or else you would be sitting in jail until your trial started."

"Thank you." Riley said to Jake as she reached him. "I'm glad somebody believes that I'm innocent."

"Oh, don't get your hopes up with him," Dominique tells her as she smirks at Jake's impassive face. "He just naturally assumes everybody is guilty – of something or another."

Riley looked from Jake to Dominique "What about you? Do you think I'm guilty?"

Dominique smiled at her. "Not at all. I'm paid to assume all of my clients are innocent. Whether they are, or not."

"But I am!"

"Of course you are," Dominique said. "And don't you say otherwise. Or you'll make my job twice as hard as it already is."

Turning back to Jake, who hasn't moved except to arch an eyebrow at them since they first walked up to him, Dominique leaned close and kissed him on the cheek. "I've done my part. Now you do yours."

Dominique turned back to Riley and looked her straight in the eye. "You can trust him. He's one of the good guys."

Turning to leave the two of them standing there, she paused long enough to tell Jake. "You know how to get a hold of me if you need me." Then spinning on her heels she slipped past Jake's car and darted across the busy street to jump into a silver Lamborghini parked directly across from him.

Barely pausing to glance over her shoulder at the on-coming traffic Dominique gunned her engine and launched herself into the stream of cars racing past. Watching her disappear into the flow of luxury cars Riley shook her head at Jake. "Doesn't anybody in this country drive a normal car?"

Shrugging at her he stepped away from his own car and opened the passenger door for her. "Depends upon what's your definition of 'normal'," he said as he gestured for her to climb into the passenger seat.

When she hesitated, he glanced at her. "What's the matter?"

"It's so low that if I get in it, I don't know whether I'll be able to get out again or not."

"Well," Jake tells her with a shrug. "It's either this or walk."

"To where?"

Jake glanced over the top of his car to the police building behind her. "Away from here."

Following his gaze Riley gave a small shudder and then turned back to him. Giving him a decisive nod she climbed into the low slung passenger seat. "Let's get out of here."

Closing her door he grinned at her. "Smart decision."

~~~

Riley relaxed into the seat as Jake climbed in beside her and eased the Ferrari into the flow of traffic passing on *rue Louis Notari*. The sun-warmed leather seat felt as smooth and supple as silk against her tired body. Momentarily closing her eyes against the late afternoon sun, a small sigh of relief escaped her lips. She has been running on adrenaline and cold coffee since waking up in the hospital more than 36 hours ago. Until this very moment, settled back into the cradle of black leather cocooning her, Riley hadn't really realized how utterly drained she felt. Since first learning about the deadly fire, she hadn't had a single moment to mourn the loss of the two people who had welcomed her to Monaco six months ago.

Not only had Carmela been a wonderful cook, she always had a smile for everyone. And others may have thought of Étienne Devereux as a ruthless international financier. But over the months as his nurse she had come to know and personally like the man. If for no other reason than the fact that even after more than thirty years of marriage, he still adored his wife. Based on what a disaster her own marriage had turned out to be, as far as she was concerned, Étienne's devotion to Constanza was worth far more than the billions of dollars people said he had. And to be truthful, from what little she saw, Constanza was far more ruthless than Étienne when it came to getting what she wanted. But, then again, maybe she was just being jealous of the woman because her marriage had been built on trust, not lies and deception.

"Can we get into the penthouse?" she asked from behind still closed eyes as Jake deftly slid around slower moving vehicles.

"No."

As her eyes flew open Riley turned to him. "But I have to. Everything I own is in my room." She stared at his chiseled profile. She hadn't noticed his after shave before now. She couldn't quite place the scent but it reminded her of riding through a high mountain forest after a spring rain.

Fresh, clean, and relaxed.

All the things she was not.

"I really want to get out of these clothes. And I need my bank card to get cash from the ATM so I can rent a hotel room for a few days."

"Sorry," he said as he swung around a white Mercedes limousine with smoky black windows. "It's still a crime scene."

"And besides that," he pointed through the windshield as they rocketed along the busy boulevard fronting the Banque de Monaco building.

Instantly recognizing the building, Riley followed his lead and glanced through the windshield towards the roof of the building expecting to see the scorched penthouse. Instead she found a sky bound mini-Ground Zero.

"What in the world…?"

As the building whipped past them and disappeared in the rear view mirror she turned back to him. "Why did it burn like that? The fire system was state of the art."

Jake nodded in agreement. "But it was disabled. Just like the security system. And the walls were steel-lined. So that turned the whole place into a blast furnace once the fire took hold."

"Why were the walls lined like that? We were four storeys up."

Jake shrugged at her. "For security."

"From what? A missile attack?"

Again Jake shrugged as he threw a quick glance into the passenger side mirror and then darted into the right lane before the gap between the two cars paralleling them had a chance to narrow. "That and electronic penetrations."

"You mean listening devices?"

He cocked his right eyebrow at her.

"I was a combat Army nurse before I took this job you know."

"Yes. That did come up in your background check."

She shook her head at him before turning her attention to the streets around them. "So what am I supposed to do?"

He shot her a quick glance as she continued. "Without my bank card I can't access my account."

"Not a problem. I've got a place."

Riley started to shake her head 'no' but Jake cut her off. "It's a company apartment. We've got several of them available for our clients. You'll have privacy and 24 hour security."

"But I'm not one of your clients." She looked around at the streets flashing past her side window. "So, if you don't mind, just drop me off at the American Attaché's office and I'll take it from there."

"I don't think so.

"I beg your pardon?"

He shot a quick glance over at her. "We have unfinished business we need to deal with."

"Oh," Riley said shifting uncomfortably in her seat. "Your bond money."

"Among other things."

"What other things?"

Instead of answering her Jake checked his rear view mirror. Satisfied no one was following them, he suddenly wheeled into the driveway leading to a gleaming high-rise building overlooking Monaco's new harbor. Pulling up to the front entrance Riley spotted the doorman instantly moving towards them. As the jacketed doorman rushed over to open Riley's door, Jake came around the front of the car and handed him the car keys and a folded bill.

"*Bon jour, M'sieur* Rafferty."

"Thanks, Michel."

Grabbing Riley's elbow, Jake hurried her inside a lobby filled with tasteful conversation areas. As he guided her directly towards the elevators, she jerked her arm free.

"I can walk by myself, thank you."

Jake merely smiled in response as he punched the elevator button. As he did, Riley glanced around uneasily.

"Look, I really appreciate you bailing me out of jail. But I think it would be better if I just got a hotel room instead."

"Not in Monaco," Jake said as the elevator arrived and he guided her into the waiting car. "Do you have any idea what the going rate is for a hotel around here?"

"I don't have to stay in Monaco. There are cheaper hotels along the coast."

As the elevator door slid closed, Jake ran a plastic security card through the electronic scanner. "Staying in Monaco is one of the terms of your bail."

Pushing the button for the Penthouse, he turned to face her. "Besides, it's hard to check into a place when you're dead."

"Dead?"

Jake glanced over at the control panel as the floor numbers on the indicator panel flashed in rapid succession. "Why do you think the paparazzi weren't waiting for you when you walked out of the police station?"

Riley blinked at him in surprise. "Why would they be interested in me? Devereux was the celebrity, not me. I'm just a nurse."

The car glided to a smooth halt and the doors slide open to reveal a small, modern private foyer serving two penthouse suites. "It has nothing to do with being a celebrity," Jake said.

He indicated for Riley to precede him out of the car. Then he stepped around her and approached the nearest suite. Inserting a second security card into the palm-sized security panel located to the right of the double engraved bronze doors, he continued. "You're the sole survivor of the fire that killed one of the richest men in Monaco."

As the door lock released, he looked down at her. "So, that makes you an instant celebrity as far as the press is concerned.

Gently opening the door he paused momentarily. "And the fact that you survived the fire also makes you the prime target for whoever it was that killed Étienne Devereux."

CHAPTER 6

"You've thrown a major monkey wrench into somebody's plan by surviving that fire," Jake continued as he stepped back so that Riley could precede him into the gleaming chrome and glass-walled penthouse suite. Polished black marble floors and ceiling, punctuated by white linen walls, framed the floor-to-ceiling glass walls that enclosed three sides of the cantilevered room overlooking Monaco's largest harbor. Sleek chrome and black leather furniture filled the room. Just beyond the far glass wall laid a floating balcony wrapped in bronze filigree.

As Jake paused at the door to reset the security system, Riley instantly spotted a pair of familiar faces – the blond Apollo Zane and his American teammate Max Stetson. They were part of the security team at the penthouse. She occasionally ran into them in the kitchen when they were on a rare coffee break. Judging from the size of their bulging muscles, she figured that they both must live in the gym when they weren't on duty guarding Étienne and Constanza. From talking to them, she knew that Apollo was from Athens and Max grew up in Seattle. And that both were ex-military and had done tours in Iraq and Afghanistan just like her. Only they had been commandos.

They both stood up when Jake turned away from the door and headed towards them with Riley at his side.

"Hey Riley," Zane said smiling at her. "It's good to see you again."

"Glad you made it out OK," Max added.

"We expected you at least 40 minutes ago," said a clipped British voice to her left.

Glancing in the direction of the voice, Riley saw a man and woman approaching from the open doorway of an ultra modern kitchen. Behind them she caught a flash of frosted glass and gleaming black granite countertops accented with lively red appliances before the lacquered door swung closed.

She recognized the wiry man moving towards them. Carmela Paulino had told her he was Jake's deputy the first time she had seen him at the penthouse. Although she had never said more than "good morning" to him a couple of time in passing, as he was either arriving or leaving the penthouse, she did know his name was Derrick Sommers. And that he and Jake Rafferty were both ex MI-6 agents who had been in the British SAS together.

She had been surprised that Rafferty had been in the British Special Forces unit. Sommers was just a little over an inch taller than her. But Jake had a good eight inches on her. And she knew that the military Special Forces units preferred shorter, more wiry men because they usually had better agility, stamina, and coordination than their taller counterparts.

Étienne Devereux had shared their background information with her when she first started working for him. He was very impressed with the fact that he had two former MI-6 agents working for him. And he was even more impressed that Jake Rafferty wasn't just a former spy. Or that he had been a member of one of the most elite military units around.

Riley quickly learned that what had most impressed this son of a Marseilles fisherman wasn't the fact that, through his own hard work, he had become one of the richest men in Europe who could afford to hire men like Jake Rafferty and Derrick Sommers. Instead, he was most impressed by the fact that Jake was the heir to a British Duke who had decided to earn his own way in life, rather than just live off of his family's long held wealth.

"Me," Étienne had admitted to her that day. "If I had been born with a silver spoon in my mouth like that, I guarantee you that I would not have ever hesitated to sit back and enjoy being that rich."

"No you wouldn't have," she remembered telling him. "Because then you wouldn't be who you are today. And you wouldn't have met your wife."

"Go on, admit it," he said as she had finished giving him his daily vitamin injection. "You're at least impressed I've got the son of a real Duke on my payroll."

"No more than I am that you have the daughter of a successful cattle rancher on that payroll as well."

Devereux had laughed heartily at that and told her with a genuine twinkle in his eye. "I like you Nurse Cooper. You're honest and you're not afraid of hard work. Just like me."

As Riley blinked away that memory, Sommers and his companion reached her side at the same time as Jake. The woman had a mane of thick mahogany-colored hair that swept her shoulders and lovely hazel eyes filled with flecks of emerald green and shiny gold.

She offered Riley her hand and a welcoming smile. "I'm Claudine Reynard. I handle all of the computer work for the team," she said with the merest trace of a French accent.

Like her, the woman was willowy but Riley could tell just by her handshake that she was strong. "Were you in the military too? Like the rest of us?" Riley asked as Claudine gazed directly into her eyes.

"*Non*," Claudine smiled and shook her head in reply.

"Actually, Claudine is the only non-military vet here," Derrick Sommers explained. "She used to be with Interpol."

When Riley turned her glance towards him, he continued. "Miss Cooper, I can't tell you how sorry we are that we weren't there for you and the others."

Riley wasn't in the mood for an apology. It was as useful as trying to stop a stampede with a cat's whisker. "Just tell me one thing. Who decided that all of you had to accompany Constanza to the dinner that night? Her or her husband?"

Derrick momentarily arched an eyebrow at Jake standing next to Riley, before he answered her question. "Her husband."

"Did you know she was wearing a fake copy of her necklace?"

"Not until later." Derrick admitted.

Shaking his head, he looked her in the eye as he continued, "much later."

"They've already answered all of these questions for Moreau," Jake tells her as his team takes in the rigid set of her face and the growing anger in her eyes.

She snapped her head around to glare at him. "What kind of professionals are you? If you were supposed to be guarding Étienne Devereux, there should have been at least one of you at the penthouse that night."

Riley moved away from Jake and the others. The anger she had been holding in check for the past several days had finally found a crack in the tight armor she had cast around her emotions to keep herself from falling apart, since first hearing the awful news about the deadly fire. Jake's people should have been there, that was their job. She should have been there, that was her job.

Ignoring Jake and the looks his people were exchanging with him, she began to pace. She had to move or she was going to blow her top and say something she shouldn't.

She didn't really have anything to do with the folks on the security team. Aside from an occasional "hello" in the kitchen or hallway, she really didn't know any of them since she had almost no contact at all with them. Unlike her relationship with her fellow nurse Bill Larson.

Not that they really had much of a relationship when you think about it. The only thing they had in common was the fact that they were both Americans and nurses who had both been in the Army. But Bill had been an enlisted medic stationed out of Fort Bragg, North Carolina which was home to the Army's Green Berets and Special Forces units. On the other hand ,she had been a Captain and a registered nurse who had served three tours in two combat theatres.

Bill hadn't gotten his nursing degree until after he finished his four-year tour at Bragg. Then he had only worked in a nursing home in Raleigh until he stumbled across the recruiting ad for the Devereux job. And the only reason he managed to land the job was because Étienne Devereux liked the idea of having ex-military nurses on his staff because they had weapons training. That meant he had an added layer of protective security around him in addition to Jake's people.

But Jake's people were all off enjoying a night at that stupid palace when they should have been there to protect him. And Bill Larson had the night off. Not that he would have been much help if he had been there. Over the months of working with him and listening to him talk, she knew he had the tendency to exaggerate when it came to his abilities and his background.

But who was she to talk. When it came to that night, she was obviously off somewhere too. Totally oblivious to the fact that her patient was dying from smoke inhalation just a few yards away from where she was.

And speaking of where she was. Why can't she remember a single thing about how she ended up with a date rape drug in her system?

The more her thoughts chased themselves around and around in a circle, the longer her strides became as the path she was pacing quickly expanded to give her room to outrun the turmoil spewing to the surface.

Seeing her mounting distress, Claudine started to reach out to her, "Riley?"

But Jake stopped her with a touch on her right arm. When she glanced over at him, he silently shook his head at her. Throwing a quick glance at Riley caught up in her inner battle Jake silently indicated the entry door, signaling his team to leave.

Nodding in understanding they all quietly followed Derrick's lead and slipped out of the penthouse. The second the door closed behind them Jake cut off Riley's pacing by stepping in front of her.

"The engineers have asked me to speak to you," he said.

"What?"

"You're wearing a hole in the floor," he said as she blinked twice and refocused on the empty room around them. "I know that you're upset and afraid, but you don't have to worry.

"You're safe here," he continued.

This time when she blinked Riley eyes lasered in on his face just inches from hers.

"Safe?" she said as if she couldn't believe he had said that to her.

Taking a step back from him she squared her shoulder and glared at him.

In an instant he saw her distracted look flash to one of scalding intensity.

"Afraid? You think I'm afraid?"

"It's understandable given what you've been through these past couple of days. And then being told that you're now the prime target for whoever is behind Devereux's death."

She let out a sharp bark of a laugh. "You don't have a clue."

She shook her head at him. "You really don't, do you?"

He gives her a slight non-committal shrug as she continued to shake her head in disbelief at him.

"You've got it completely wrong," she said. "I'm not afraid."

She glared at him.

"I'm furious."

From the anger in her eyes he had no doubt that she's telling the truth. Angry was good. That meant he could make use of it.

"What are you angry about?"

In the blink of an eye she went from angry to incredulous.

"You can't be serious?"

He folded his arms and waited for her to continue.

"I'm a nurse. A patient died on my watch."

He nodded at her in encouragement.

"Not only did my patient die, but so did a co-worker who was a good friend to me."

As the anger began to build again, Riley started to stalk around the perimeter of the room while Jake's eyes keep pace with her. "Somebody did that just so they could steal a stupid necklace."

"It wasn't stupid," Jake said. "That necklace is worth $157 million to whoever has it."

Riley paused to glare over her shoulder at him rooted next to the coffee table composed of a four-foot long, twisted ovoid purple geode supporting a sheet of tempered glass. "What difference does that make?"

She resumed her pacing. "It was still just a necklace."

She shook her head in frustration. "And two people died because of it."

"True," Jake said as she moved along the wall of sunlit glass. For some reason she made him think of a lioness on the hunt as she stalked across the wide expanse of the room.

"But it is worth a good-sized fortune And for some people, that's worth killing for," he continued.

"Not for me. No price is worth a human life."

Jake shrugged at her. "Not everyone shares your values."

Reaching the far wall, Riley's path was bringing her back in his direction. "Sharing my values has nothing to do with it." Again she shook her head in frustration. "I screwed up."

She looked over at him with a face now filled with pain.

"And two people I cared about died."

"That wasn't your fault," Jake told her sharply. "We both know that you were unconscious when that fire started." It was his turn to shake his head. "If anyone screwed up here, it was me."

"Why you? You weren't even in town." She returned to his side. "Étienne was the one who decided he didn't need or want any security that night. That wasn't your fault"

Jake gave her a half shrug of his shoulders.

"And Étienne was the boss. So what could your people do when he insisted that they all had to accompany Constanza to the Palace?"

He slowly nods in agreement. "All right, I'll accept that." Cocking his head slightly, he continues. "So what are you furious about? As head of Security if I'm not responsible, then neither are you."

Standing this close to her he couldn't help noticing how thick her eyelashes were. Before she could answer the question – or he could stop to think about it – Jake pulled her to him and brushed his lips lightly across her startled lips.

Then as her eyes melted into a dreamy distance he dived deeper into the warmth of the kiss.

Against her will Riley's eyes fluttered as a tingling current swept through her whole body causing her knees to almost buckle with pleasure. Her eyes and knees weren't the only parts of her fluttering as the tip of Jake's tongue parted her lips and tasted all of her. She didn't know why he decided to kiss her. Or why she was returning his kiss. She only knew that here and now she was being pulled deeper and deeper into the well of his male magnetism. And the deeper she went the faster the anger was flowing out of her.

And that was good because here she didn't have to think.

Here all she had to do was feel.

Safe.

Protected.

Wanted.

CAROL A. HUGHES

CHAPTER 7

"No!"

Riley blinked hard and pulled back.

He wanted her all right. Just like Mark had wanted her too.

To take what she had so he could walk away with the prize.

Her ranch.

Information about what happened at the penthouse.

But not this time. This time she refused to be duped again.

This time she was going to be the one walking away with the prize. This time she was going to do what the police and Jake Rafferty didn't seem to be able to do. She was going to find out who killed Étienne Devereux. She was going to clear her name and walk away from this place with her head held high. Never again would she crawl away with her tail between her legs like a whooped coyote.

Someone wanted her dead. And all Jake Rafferty really cared about was saving the reputation of his company since it was their fault Étienne and Carmela had died. She knew his trick. He thought he could use his good looks and charm to worm information out of her about Étienne and Carmela's killer. Or worse yet, to use her as bait to dangle for the killer.

Well, it wasn't going to work.

Not this time.

Glaring at him she moved around the end of the coffee table. "Why did you do that?"

Jake fought to get his heart rate back under control. Good question he thought. Was he out of his bloody mind pulling a stunt like that? She was an asset – a very important asset - and here he is acting like a horny schoolboy.

And where did that come from? He hadn't been physically drawn to a single woman since Lily. And this woman didn't bear the slightest resemblance to Lily. So why in the world was his libido suddenly going wonkers on him like this?

"I'm sorry. I was out of line."

"'Out of line'?" Riley glared at him. "You were so far over the line that you are at least two counties over."

"You are completely right," Jake said.

"So why did you do it?"

Jake shook his head at her. "I honestly don't know what came over me. All I can do is to offer you my deepest apology. And assure you that it won't happen again."

He watched her glaring at him from her side of the glass table.

"Did you assume that bailing me out of jail entitled you to certain liberties?"

Riley saw Jake unexpectedly blink in surprise before he quickly slid a mask of neutrality over his face. "Of course not," he said shaking his head at her.

"Then why did you bail me out?" she asked. "My fingerprints were all over the bottle of alcohol used to start the fires. I was in the position to turn off all the alarm systems.

She fisted both her hands that were hanging by her sides. "You know as well as I do that Bill Larson wasn't the only one who took the job with the Devereuxes because he needed the money."

She locked eyes with him. "*Inspecteur* Moreau knew all about my ex-husband stealing my family's ranch from me in our divorce. So I'm assuming that you and your people did too."

Jake gives her a slight nod in agreement.

"Forget the fact that I know less than zero about fencing a stolen necklace worth millions." She shook her head at him as she continued. "But I'll admit that I certainly could have used the money for lawyers."

She started pacing again. Only this time her movements were deliberate, thoughtful. Not frantic like they had been earlier.

"So I can understand why the police are looking at me sideways."

She stopped moving to look over at him. "But you and your people have been watching me on your security monitors ever since I arrived. Surely you can see that I would never harm Étienne or Carmela. That I would never hurt anyone."

She took a step towards him in order to drive home her point. "I'm a nurse. I heal people. I don't kill them."

Jake wanted to believe her. And she had been right about them watching her on the security monitors since her arrival at the penthouse. He knew for a fact that both Apollo and Max had given her positive marks in their weekly staff reports. While they thought her fellow American was a jerk personality-wise as far as his dealings with the rest of the staff went. But he was technically competent according to the Devereuxes' head nurse, Silvia Longazini.

Jake had personally raised the issue with Étienne Devereux a few months after Larson's arrival. But the old man thought Larson was "entertaining." And he had two other things going in his favor. He was the only male nurse on the staff. Which was helpful when it came time to do any heavy lifting, according to both Étienne and Silvia. Plus the fact that he did have weapons training thanks to his four years in the Army. So Devereux didn't care whether or not the staff liked him. He did and that's all that mattered since he was calling the shots.

"I didn't have any reason in the world to kill them," Riley said when he didn't immediately reply to her.

He knew from their background checks that both Larson and Riley took the job because Devereux was paying them three times their normal rate. Larson definitely needed the money because he was in trouble with the U.S. taxman. He was also two years behind in child support payments to an ex-wife. And unless he kept up his monthly payments, he was facing a jail term back home. The only problem with Larson as a suspect as the insider for the job was the fact that he had a solid alibi for that night.

As far as Riley losing her family ranch to her ex-husband during their divorce. Max had learned from the dead cook that she was saving her salary so she could afford to hire a lawyer to help her get it back.

"But you did have a reason," he said. "And you were there when the whole thing went down."

The blood drained from her face in shock from his clearly unexpected reply. Then it flooded back like the rush of a crimson tide as the anger blazed in her eyes.

"I most certainly did not have a reason," she said shaking her head back in forth in adamant denial. "In fact, with Étienne dead I'm out of a job."

She glared at him. "A very good paying job as you well know."

"You won't need it if you had Constanza's necklace."

"Which I don't!"

Ignoring her angry denial he continued. "You won't be able to collect the full value on it. But a good fence with the right connections might be able to get you at least $100 million for it."

He watched the fury boiling in her face as he calmly continued. "Of course they'll have to break up the diamond and reset the entire necklace to hide its true identity."

Her jaws ached from clenching her teeth so tight. Temper, girl. This jerk is going to believe what he wants to believe. No matter what you tell him. So stop being as stupid as him and do what he's doing. Use him like he's using you.

Pulling air all the way into the very bottom of her lungs and then slowly exhaling Riley unclenched her jaw and rotated her head in a circle to unlock her cramped neck muscles. She did this five times until her temper was reduced to a mere memory. Licking her cracked lips to wet them, she raised her head and smiled at Jake.

"I'm not stupid you know."

"I've never thought you were."

"And believe it or not, I do understand where you're coming from."

"Oh?" he said arching his right eyebrow at her.

She nodded pleasantly at him. "Uh-hnn. It ticks me off, but there's nothing I can do about it."

"About what?"

"The fact that you and *Inspecteur* Moreau both think I had something to do with what happened. From your perspective it is a logical suspicion."

"I'm glad to see that we finally agree on something here."

"Oh, I don't 'agree' with you. In fact, I most definitely don't agree with you at all," she said.

"Especially since I know for a fact that it's not true." She flashed the briefest of smiles at him as she continued. "But for now why don't we both just agree to disagree. And move forward from here."

"All right," Jake said, warily watching her facial movements. She was good when it came to controlling her temper judging by the friendly smile she was aiming at him. She was smart enough to realize that her emotions weren't helping her cause. He had to at least give her credit for that.

She clearly thought that she was going to play him. So why not see how she intended to do it. "How do you see us moving forward on this? Seeing as how you keep insisting that you cannot remember anything about most of that day."

Giving him a half shrug she strolled around to his side of the coffee table and causally sat down at the far end of the sofa. "You're the pro here. I'm just the bait, remember?"

Giving him a sardonic smile, she continued. "This is your game. So why don't you tell me what your game plan is."

"But as the bait, you do have to agree that I do bring a certain cachet to mix," she added. Cocking her head to the right she looked up at his standing at his end of the couch. "So, before you get started, we need to lay out some ground rules first."

An amused half smile tugged at the right corner of Jake's mouth as he joined her on the sofa. Resting his back against the arm rest at his end, he gestured for her to continue.

Nodding back in acceptance Riley began by holding up her forefinger. "Firstly, based upon the lab's discovery of the Rohypnol in my blood stream, it's a supportable conclusion that I was indeed unconscious at the time the fire started."

Jake was curious how far she intended to take this. "OK, that's reasonable."

"Secondly," she said as her eyes lasered in on his face. "We don't know when the necklace was stolen."

"It was stolen that night. We were able to confirm its presence in the penthouse the evening before the fires."

Riley shook her head at him. "That's not what I meant."

"Then what do you mean?"

"We don't know if it was taken before or after the fires were started."

"And that is important because . . . ?"

"You can believe this or not," Riley said. "But I honestly didn't know there was a safe in the penthouse. And that was because I never gave it a thought. I just presumed that the Devereuxes kept all of their valuables downstairs in the bank's vault since Étienne owned the bank."

"On your ranch, did you have a safe?" Jake asked her. "For keeping your payroll and important papers?"

Puzzled where he going with his question, Riley nodded at him, "Yes."

"Then why wouldn't you'd think that the Devereuxes, with all of their money and jewels, won't do the same thing?"

"Because," she snapped at him. "We didn't live upstairs from a bank we owned."

Swallowing his grin at her temper flare-up, Jake said, "OK, that makes sense."

As the rigidity went out of her spine he continued, "So what is your point here?"

"Just because I was clueless about the house safe that doesn't mean other people on the staff were. Especially those who had been working there longer than I had."

Of course they had considered that from the start. But he wanted to keep her talking to see if he could pick up any information at all from her that he could use. "Anybody in particular?"

Riley shifted uncomfortably before answering. "I'm not accusing anybody, you understand?"

"Of course you aren't," he said soothingly.

She shot him an annoyed look. "Please don't patronize me like that. I'm just trying to work out logically who else on the staff, besides me, could have possibly been involved."

"Why do you think it was someone on the staff?"

"Somebody shut off the alarms before they could go off. And that had to be done from inside of the penthouse."

"True."

"There was only Carmela and I on duty. I know for sure I didn't do it."

"So that leaves Carmela or Devereux himself."

She shook her head at him. "I just can't see Étienne Devereux deliberately turning off his alarm system. Especially given his fear of being kidnapped or attacked by some of the folks he had been doing business with in the Middle East."

"Yet he sent the entire security team to the Palace with his wife," Jake pointed out to her.

"Yes, he did. I don't know why. But I'm guessing that he felt secure knowing how good his alarm system was."

"But someone could have gotten in and grabbed him before the cops could have responded to the alarms since the house team was gone," Jake said.

"True. But he knew I was a crack shot before I went into the Army. I had told him about all of the shooting contest blue ribbons I won growing up."

She shook her head at Jake as she continued. "And he knew that I was on duty that night. So maybe that's what lulled him into a false sense of security."

Riley turned slightly towards Jake who had not taken his eyes off her face since they had been talking. "Maybe that's why he thought it was OK to send your guys away that night?"

"It's possible." Jake agreed. "But since we are never going to be able to confirm that, don't beat yourself up over it. Étienne is the one who made the decision that he did."

"And he's the one who died because of that decision," Riley replied in a voice filled with pain.

"If you didn't have anything to do with what happened," Jake began. But Riley cut him off before he could continue.

"I didn't!"

"Okay," Jake continued in a calm voice. "Since you were not involved in what happened that night, then you have no reason to be blaming yourself for Devereux's death."

"You don't understand," Riley said jumping up from the sofa to stare down at him. "He was my patient. It was my responsibility to protect him."

Standing up Jake crossed over to her side and pitched his voice low. "Whoever was involved were professionals. I don't care how many shooting blue ribbons you won as a kid. Believe me when I tell you, you would have never stood a chance against them. I've seen the results of their work before. Whoever they were, they were definitely professionals. And they are definitely killers."

"How do you know that?" Riley said as she tried to swallow the pain in her throat.

"Because I used to be one of them."

CHAPTER 8

"Well it's clear that they've definitely had some kind of kind of commando training," Riley said.

She was quicker on her feet than he expected. "What makes you say that?"

Riley instantly narrowed her eyes at him as she looked to see whether or not his question was sincere. Returning his steady gaze she decided to continue. As she talked, she tapped her fingers as she ticked off her points.

"Firstly, there's no way either one of us is going to believe that they just happened to hit the penthouse on the one night there wasn't a single security team member present inside the place."

Jake gave her a clipped nod in agreement. "Which means?"

"Which means," Riley said looking him in the eye, "they had good recon."

"You're a nurse. What do you know about reconnaissance?"

Riley instantly honed in on the whisper of condescendence tingeing Jake's question. Tightening her jaw to contain the sudden flare of her temper, she told him coldly, "You'd be surprise what you learn after three tours in a combat zone. Especially when you're medivacing wounded commandos out of hot zones."

She may have been answering calmly, but Jake could feel the heat of her anger as she glowered at him. Watching her work with Devereux, he had never realized just how feisty she could be. That was definitely a good thing because it would make his job a lot easier. Of course it just might make it harder instead.

Giving her a slight nod of acknowledgement he said, "Point taken. But common criminals could do the same thing."

"True," Riley agreed. "But not only did they hit the place when there wasn't any security presence inside the penthouse. They also managed to breach all of the security systems without triggering a single alarm."

"That wasn't hard to do since the security system had been shut down."

Riley shook her head at him. "In the penthouse, yes. But not for the rest of the building."

She was right, Jake thought as she continued with a satisfied smile on her face.

"So we're looking at common criminals who had some kind of commando training."

Jake was curious. "Why 'common criminals'? They could have been terrorists or an assassin squad going after Devereux."

She shook her head at him. "They weren't interested in Étienne."

Jake was definitely intrigued by where she was going with this. "What makes you think that? He was worth give or take a few billion. Constanza would have paid any ransom they asked."

Again Riley shook her head in response. "Étienne wasn't the target. The necklace was."

Jake considered her point and then gave her a slight shrug in reply.

What is it with men, Riley thought when she saw the half shrug he gave her. They just hate to admit it when a woman out thinks them. She knew darn well that Jake and his people had all assumed that Étienne was the prime target of the attack.

"What makes you think they were after the necklace and not Devereux?" Jake interrupted her thoughts.

Now it was her turn to return the half shrug. "If they were good enough to get in without triggering a single alarm, then they were good enough to get him out of the place undetected as well."

She looked him in the eye as she continued, "Moreau told me he died of smoke inhalation. Is that true?"

Jake nodded in reply. "According to the autopsy."

"And that you found him in bed and undisturbed. Right?"

"Yes."

Riley gestured with her right hand as she replied, "Then it's clear they weren't interested in him. If they had time to locate and open the house safe and grab the necklace, then they also had time to snatch Étienne for ransom as well."

She shook her head at Jake. "But they didn't." Distress hitched her voice as she continued, "Instead they left him to die."

"Just like they did you and Carmela?"

"You know Devereux had some very powerful enemies," Jake continued. "He was doing a lot of business in the Middle East. As a financier, he didn't take sides in the various conflicts going on there. Instead, he financed both sides."

"So some of those people would have either wanted him dead for helping fund their enemies," Riley said as Jake moved over to the glass wall overlooking the sun lit harbor at the base of the high rise.

"Or else they could have done what he was in constant fear of," she continued as Jake let the sunlight streaming through the glass warm his shoulders. "They could have kidnapped him for ransom."

Riley crosses the room to join him in the sunlight. "But they didn't attempt to do either. And they certainly had the time."

She was facing the harbor below. Turning her head to the left she to look at Jake, she continues. "If that is what they had wanted to do, neither Carmela or I could have stopped them."

Jake turned his head to look at her as she turned her gaze out through the glass. Even from her profile he can see the pain and guilt on her face.

"That wasn't your job," he said. "It was mine."

Letting out the breath she had been holding in, and swallowing the egg-sized lump in her throat, Riley turned slightly to face him as he continued in a soft voice.

"You have nothing to feel guilty about. You didn't fail. I did."

Giving him a slight shake of her head, Riley blinked away the sheen of tears that had come out of nowhere on her. "But you weren't there. I was. I should have been able to save them.

"It was my watch and both of them died." Shaking her head in distress she turned away from him. "I didn't do anything to help them."

"Says who?" Jake demanded.

Puzzled, Riley glanced up as he moved in front of her. Gently grabbing her by her upper arms, Jake forced her to look at him as a new sheen of moisture threatened to turn into full-fledged tears on her.

"You had almost made it to Devereux's master suite when I found you unconscious in the hallway."

He continued as she blinked in surprise. "The place was an inferno. And you had every right to head for the exit." He gave her a gentle shake to underscore his words. "But you didn't."

He looked her straight in the eyes as he said, "You almost died trying to save Devereux."

"But Carmela?" she whispered.

Jake shook his head at her. "She was killed by a blow to the head. Whoever killed her was expecting the fire to mask the injury.

"There was nothing you – or anyone else – could have done to save either one of them." Jake gave her a stern look. "You were in no way responsible for their deaths."

The relief that flooded through Riley at his words left her as weak as if she had run a marathon. Just as she opened her mouth to thank him for telling her that, he slammed her with a left hook that she never saw coming when he said, "Unless you were the one behind the Rohypnol injection."

Jake had seen the relief wash through Riley at his opening comment. But he had a job to do if he was going to uncover the truth behind Étienne Devereux's death. He owed the man at least that since he hadn't been there to save his life like he should have.

In a flash that flood of relief vanished from her eyes as she jerked away from his hold.

"You son-of-a-...," she shook with rage as she swallowed the rest of her words.

He could easily imagine her breathing fire as she glared at him. "You're as bad as Inspector Moreau."

Stomping across the room to the leather couch she whirled around and continued to glare at him. "I'm only going to say this one more time. And then that's it.'

"I."

"Did."

"Not."

"Inject."

"Myself."

"With."

"Anything."

"At - All."

"Period!"

He watched her fist her hands and cross them under her armpits. Then stare across the distance separating them with a look of pure fury on her face.

"Got that?" she demanded.

He let her fume for a full minute before making the next move in his gambit. Anger either sharpened one's wits. Or, it turned them into an idiot. Now he was about to find out which side of the plate she fell off of.

She had been one of three people inside that penthouse when the invasion took place. As the sole survivor, she was the only asset that he and his team could put into play in order to pick up the trail they needed. She had been spot on about the fact that whoever had hit the penthouse weren't just ordinary criminals. And she had also picked up on what he and Moreau hadn't. There was a higher than average chance that the necklace has actually been the target of the attack – not Étienne Devereux.

Based upon what had gone down inside the penthouse, he knew that he was definitely dealing with pros who had the same training as he and his team. They were in and out in record time. They had been able to infiltrate the site without triggering a single alarm. They definitely had insider info on the layout of the site. So the identity of that insider was the key to picking up their trail.

The question was if Riley wasn't their inside contact – then who was it?

Riley, the cook and Devereux were the only ones inside the penthouse when Constanza Devereux left with the security team. The penthouse's security perimeter was intact when they left. The Security Control Room was sealed and only his people had the door code. And according to the hospital's lab report Riley was unconscious by then.

So did the cook open the door to the intruders? Or was an intruder somehow hidden inside already when Derrick and the others left for the charity dinner? And if he was, who let him in and when? If the cook wasn't the one then Riley could have done it before she was drugged like Moreau suspected.

Just as Moreau had done, Jake had reviewed the building's security tapes and found no sign of anyone entering the penthouse after Derrick and the team left with Constanza Devereux. The male nurse, Bill Larson, was visible on the tapes as he left the building twenty minutes after his shift ended. Just as he reported to the police when they questioned him the morning after the deadly fire.

The roof of the penthouse was wired and was under 24-hour video surveillance from both Jake's and the building's own monitors. Both the roof and Jake's security tapes were completely destroyed by the fire. But the building's video feed was backed up and undamaged. And the only thing it revealed were the flames erupting through the metal lined roof before the flames destroyed all of the roof-mounted cameras.

So the question remained – how did the intruders manage to breach the penthouse's security perimeter without leaving a single trace of their presence on any of the various video cameras installed throughout the entire building?

Even though the fire damage from the blaze had completely destroyed the entire penthouse, Jake knew from the arson investigator that the safe had not been torched or blown to open it. Instead, the intruders had used an digital code scanner on the electronic keypad. That meant they had the safe open in a matter of seconds.

Despite her time in Iraqi and Afghanistan, Riley had been no threat to whoever was behind the attack. She had been incapacitated by the Rohypnol. The cook was barely five feet tall and probably didn't weigh a hundred pounds dripping wet and wearing bricks for shoes. And Devereux was middle-aged, fifty pounds overweight and with limited mobility due to his bad back.

None of the three of them were any threat to anyone. So why the need for the fire? Devereux and the cook could just as easily have been given the Rohypnol like Riley. With the three of them unconscious the intruders had plenty of time to make their getaway.

As for it being a hit. Sending in an entire team to take out Devereux was overkill. That could have been handled by just one man. He could have OD'd the target and one of the nurses would have taken the fall for it with no problem.

So he had to agree with Riley. The necklace as the target made more sense. One man worked the safe while a couple of others were busy setting multiple fires throughout the entire penthouse suite. One man on watch in the stairwell and one in the elevator foyer. One to secure the staff and you'd be all set. A four-man team was doable. But six would have cut down on the time on site. They could have been in, out, and gone in less than five minutes total. Two-and-a-half minutes if they had any inside help.

Knowing exactly just how good his security perimeter had been, Jake knew that the only breach possible had to have come from the inside. And like Marcel Moreau, Riley Cooper had been his prime suspect too.

Then the lab report had come in. And that had created more problems than it solved. Because now he was as confused as the police were about Riley's actual role in the attack.

Was she an innocent victim as she insisted?

Or was she something much darker?

A clever criminal who had accidentally got caught up in the fire?

Or, maybe a willing participant, whose accomplices had deliberately left her there to die?

CHAPTER 9

Riley did not like it. Not one bit.

She, the situation, her emotions and Jake Rafferty were completely out of control and all over the place. One minute she was weak-kneed and weepy because "Mr. Sexy Lips" kissed her and told her that it wasn't her fault that two people died because she didn't do her job. Then, in the very next breath he insinuates that she was actually involved with what happened.

Well he can take his good looks and cute little accent and put them back up on the shelf because they weren't going to work with her. She had already been down that particular road before and was never going there again.

And what in the world was the matter with her anyway? Did she have "FOOL" engraved on her forehead? The man had barely said a single "hello" to her in the six months that she'd been working at the penthouse. Then one of his richest clients gets killed because none of his people were where they should have been in the first place. And all of a sudden he's willing to pony up a million Euros to bail her out of jail.

Yep she definitely had "FOOL" branded right in the middle of her forehead if she thought she was anything else but very expensive bait to the man.

OK. If that was his game, she would just have to live with it. As long as it kept her out of jail and able to do what she was going to have to do to clear her own name. Because heaven knows nobody else was going to do it for her.

"What happened to the back-up copies of the security monitor tapes from the penthouse?" she said looking over at Jake.

"What?"

"Apollo mentioned one time when we were talking that you all kept copies of the tapes from the security monitors."

Jake arched an eyebrow at her as she continued. "Since everybody seems to think that maybe I had something to do with the raid on the penthouse, I'm going to have to assume that the tapes from that night were destroyed by the fire."

Jake gave her a thoughtful look before slowly nodding in response. "They were."

"But what about from earlier in the day?"

"What about earlier in the day?"

"The last thing I remember about that day was getting into the shower to get ready for my shift," she said returning his look. "I have no idea how or when I was drugged.'

Riley gave a slight shake of her head in frustration. "Or who could have done it. So I'm hoping maybe I'll see something that might jog loose a memory or two about what happened."

"Sorry," Jake said shaking his head at her. "The tapes were usually backed up to disc at midnight."

"So you have nothing from that day at all?"

"No."

Throwing her head back and momentarily staring at the ceiling in frustration Riley scrunched her lips together as her mind raced.

"Larson," she said looking over at Jake.

"What about him?"

"I need to talk to him. He would have briefed me at the end of his shift," she explained. "But I don't have any memory at all of taking a report from him that day."

"Rohypnol is very fast acting once it gets into your system," Jake knew exactly where she's going with her question. "So, if the last thing you remember is getting into the shower before you started your shift...."

"Then I must have been drugged around that time," she interrupted. "And that means I wouldn't have been in any shape to report for work," she said triumphantly as Jake nodded in agreement with her.

"Inspector Moreau said Bill left the penthouse at 7:20 that evening." Riley continued. "Since only Carmela and I were there with Devereux, that means that Larson didn't call in the back up nurse to cover for me."

She slowly shook her head back and forth at Jake, "Why didn't he?"

"Maybe Devereux told him not to."

Riley rolled her eyes at Jake. "If I was out of it, I guarantee you that Bill wouldn't have chanced going to Devereux about it."

"Why not?"

"Because he might have ended up covering my shift instead since he was already there." It was her turn to cock an eyebrow at Jake. "Believe me when I tell you that Bill Larson would never take a chance like that. The guy did as little work as he could get away with and still keep his job."

As Jake reacted, she continued, "Devereux wouldn't care about the overtime expenses. But Silvia would since she acts like our O.T. is coming directly out of her own pocket. So Bill knew as well as I do that she would have had a back-up nurse there to cover for me if she had known about me not being able to work."

Riley turned to Jake. "Silvia can't stand Bill. I know for a fact that she'd love to get rid of him, but for some reason Étienne liked him.

"But if he took off before a relief nurse got there to cover for me, Silvia would definitely use that to convince Étienne to let her fire him like she wanted to do."

"Maybe that's why he didn't call her."

Riley frowned in puzzlement so Jake explained. "If Devereux was in any pain that night, he could have given him something for it. Then took off for his night on the town."

Riley clearly wasn't fully convinced so Jake continued. "He knew Carmela was there. So could it be possible that he told her to call him if she couldn't get you to take care of the problem? That way he could avoid dealing with Silvia and still get his time off like he planned."

Pursing her lips Riley considered that scenario for a second or two and then nodded her head in agreement with him. "Yeah. That sounds exactly like what Bill would do."

Relaxing her stance slightly, Riley continued. "The Rohypnol."

"What about it?"

"Somebody drugged me," she said locking eyes with him. "So the question is – who, how and when did they do it?"

Jake returned her level gaze. "Who do you think did it?"

She shook her head in reply. "I have absolutely no idea. We didn't keep it on hand. So somebody had to have brought it in with them."

"And you don't have any idea who that could be?"

Again she shook her head in response. "Nope. Not a clue."

"What is the last clear memory you have from that day?"

Scrunching her face in thought Riley ignored Jake and slowly moved to the glass wall facing the sea. "I wasn't scheduled to go on duty until seven o'clock."

From behind her Jake nodded slightly in agreement with her comment.

"So it must have been around five when I started to get ready."

"Why so early?"

She glanced over at him. "I was going to get a quick shower and then have a light supper with Carmela in the kitchen since she didn't like to eat alone."

"Did you do that?"

Riley frowned as she tried to pull up the memories. After a moment or two she slowly shook her head back and forth in a short arc. "I don't know." She glanced back at Jake as frustration tightened her features. "I can't remember."

"That's OK. Let's focus on what you can remember."

Huffing in frustration, Riley gave him a curt nod. "Right." Then she concentrated on cutting through the fog shrouding her memories of that day.

"I remember...," she began as she focused her attention inward. "...walking into the bathroom and turning on the shower."

"Good," Jake said. "That's a start."

Riley cut her eyes over to him in warning before refocusing her attention.

"It always took a minute or two for the shower to heat up. So I grabbed my toothbrush and the paste to brush my teeth."

Jake nodded at her silently in encouragement as she slowly continued.

"It was a new tube. And I thought that was strange."

"Why?"

Riley shot him a quick look. "What?"

"Why was it strange that it was a new tube of toothpaste?"

Her brows knitted together in a slight frown as she tugged at her memories. "Because," she answered slowly as the memory started to float closer to the surface, "it should have been slightly used."

"OK, that's good," Jake encouraged her. "But you used it anyhow?"

She nodded in reply. "Yeah. Then I got into the shower because it had finally started steaming."

"Good. How long were you in the shower?"

Riley turned her head away from him as she concentrated on his question.

Seeing the frown lines deepening between her eyebrows as she struggled to come up with an answer to his simple question Jake crossed over to her side.

"Riley, how long were you in that shower?"

Looking up at him Riley shook her head in confusion. "I don't know. I can remember climbing into the tub and closing the shower door."

He nodded as she struggled to continue. "I remember turning towards the water."

Her eyes widened as she focused on his face. "And that's the last thing I remember."

"You don't remember getting out of the shower?"

She quickly shook her head at him.

"You don't remember getting dressed?"

Again she shook her head in silent response.

"Or if you went to the kitchen?"

"No," she said in a tight voice. "Nothing."

Jake took a step back and gave her an encouraging smile. "That's good."

"Why is that good?" she said as she once again shook her head in confusion.

"Because now we have a good idea of how, and when, you were drugged."

Her eyebrows drew together for a second before understanding broke across her face. "The toothpaste!"

"That would be my guess," Jake said nodding an agreement.

"But I just used a dab of it."

"That was enough to make you woozy and compliant."

She suddenly gave him a sharp look. "How well do you know your people?"

"Why?"

"Just answer the question. How well do you know your people? And do you trust them?

She was peering at him like a raptor about to attack.

"With my life," he said as anger pulled a tight circle of lines around her eyes. "Why?"

"So you're telling me that they are completely trustworthy?"

"Absolutely."

It was Riley's turn to sucker punch him. Which she did by giving him a short, satisfied nod in response to his reply. "That's my impression too."

As he regarded her warily she continued. "So that means we need to talk to Bill Larson."

"Why? Moreau checked out his alibi and it was solid. He was at the Casino with a date. They captured both of them on the Casino's security monitors."

Riley shook her head back and forth at him. "I don't care about his alibi during the fire."

Anger tightened her lips into a thin line as she glared at Jake. "What I want to know is - why did he drug me before the fire?"

CHAPTER 10

"Larson?" Jake caught the glint of anger dancing in her eyes. "What makes you think it was Larson who drugged you?

Riley was clenching her jaws so tight she could have pulverized steel between her teeth. "Because that new tube of toothpaste was not there when I brushed my teeth that morning."

She looked him in the eye as she continued. "That's why I was surprised to find a new one that afternoon. Only, at the time, I didn't realize what was off."

Jake gave her a short nod. "OK. But why do you think that Larson is the one who doctored the toothpaste?"

"Earlier that day I was in the kitchen getting a cup of coffee. When I came back to my room, I found him outside of it. And it looked to me as if he was just leaving."

"Did you confront him?"

"Yes."

"And what did he say?"

"He claimed that he had found the door open and was just closing it when I walked around the corner of the hallway."

"Was it possible that's what had happened?"

Riley gave him a curt shake of her head. "No. I didn't believe him for a minute."

"Why not?"

"Because he was pulling the door closed behind him."

She cocked her head slightly to the right as she returned Jake's gaze. "If he had really found the door open, and was just closing it as he claimed."

"Then he was facing the wrong way," Jake concluded for her.

"Exactly."

"What about Carmela?" Could she have possibly switched out the toothpaste?"

Riley surprised Jake because she actually paused to consider that possibility before she answered.

"Anything is possible. But the toothpaste was clearly the source of the Rohypnol. And that was in my room."

Jake nodded in agreement as she continued. "Larson was the one I found creeping around my room, not Carmela."

"Maybe she had been creeping around it, but you just didn't catch her."

Again Riley considered his suggestion before she decisively shook her head at him. "It's possible. But not practical."

Jake cocked a questioning eyebrow at her.

"If Carmela wanted to drug me, all she had to do was doctor my cup of coffee when I was in the kitchen. It was sitting on the counter while I was getting the creamer from the refrigerator."

When he gave her a slight shrug of acceptance, she continued. "We are talking about a $157 million diamond going missing. But since you've vouched for your people, I'm willing to take them out of the equation – for now."

"Cautious woman, aren't you?" Jake said as a hint of a smile tried to tug at the corner of his mouth.

"Yes, I am." Riley said firmly.

Jake caught the underlying determination in her voice as she continued. "Do you know if Larson is still in Monaco?"

"Why?"

"Because he owes me an explanation and a lot of answers."

Jake took in the determined set of her chin. "The police will handle him."

Rolling her eyes at him, Riley shook her head. "Yeah, sure they will. They'll question him, but not to clear my name.

Stepping back from Jake, Riley crossed her arms under her breasts and arched her own eyebrow at him. "Your Inspector Moreau is not as interested in proving me innocent, as he is in proving that I was involved in what happened."

"That's not true."

Riley lowered her chin and arched both eyebrows at him. "Sorry, buster. But that pig ain't going fly with me."

"I beg your pardon?"

Shaking her head at the ceiling overhead, Riley moved away from Jake. "He may be a friend of yours," she threw over her shoulder at him as she crossed the room. "But I can guarantee you that he's not one of mine."

Jake followed her across the room. "He's a good cop. You can trust him."

Riley swung around and glared at Jake as he reached her side. "No, I can't. I don't. And I won't."

"Well you really don't have much choice in the matter," Jake said ignoring the scowl on her face. "It's an ongoing homicide investigation and he's in charge."

Riley twitched her right shoulder at him in response. "Yeah, right. And I suppose he's going to let me sit in with him when he questions Larson."

"I'm pretty sure that the answer to that would be no."

Nodding her head in agreement, Riley stepped around Jake and started for the door.

"Where are you going?"

Never breaking stride she threw a quick glance over her shoulder as she said, "To talk to Bill Larson."

Jake hurried around her to block her exit.

"How? You don't even know where he is at the moment."

Riley was brought up short when Jake stepped between her and the front door. "Get out of my way."

"It's a fool's errand."

Riley gave him a cold stare. "More than you realize. Now please get out of my way."

Jake shook his head at her. "Sorry, but I can't let you do this. This is a police matter and they are the ones who need to deal with it. Not you."

"Excuse me?" Anger ripped through Riley faster than a runaway freight train. "Just who do you think you're talking to?"

Before he could even open his mouth to response, she continued to roll right over him as she glared daggers at him. "Do you honestly think I'm stupid enough to think that you are just going to stand around with your hands in pockets and do nothing about the fact that a client you were supposed to be protecting was viciously murdered?"

She took a slight step back so that she didn't have to crane her head back to look at him. "We both know the answer to that. So why in the world would you expect me to sit around and do nothing to clear myself as well?"

Fisting her hands and planting them on her hips she continued to confront him. "You might have a lot riding on this case being solved. But that's just business for you. In case you haven't noticed, I've got a whole lot more riding on this bronc than you do. I'm looking at a lot of years in jail for something I had nothing to do with."

She slowly shook her head back and forth two times. "And I know for a fact that I can't depend upon anybody except me when it comes to getting me out of this mess."

"That's not true," Jake said in a calm voice. "I've known Marcel Moreau for a lot of years and he's an excellent cop. If you really aren't involved, then you don't have anything to worry about. He will uncover the truth."

"'IF' I'm not involved!" Riley sputtered. Red tinged her vision for a moment as she felt the blood pounding in her ears and filling her head with a thunderous roar. The police suspecting she might be involved, that she could understand. They didn't know her. So of course it was only natural for them to be suspicious of her. But Jake Rafferty had six months of security videos on her. And he had run a background check on her when she was hired. Unlike Bill Larson, he knew she wasn't up to her eyeballs in debt. So if anybody was going to be the inside person that they suspected existed, why couldn't he and Moreau see that she wasn't exactly the best candidate for that dubious honor.

But somebody had to have been involved since the penthouse's security systems had been turned off. So she was just going to have to work with the cards in her hand. Whether she liked them or not. They just were what they were. That meant that there was no use whining about it, like her Dad used to say.

Dousing the flash of temper Riley continued. "Moreau's already got his sight set on me and he's not about to let go of that bone. Adding Bill Larson to the pot is only going to make that stew richer."

Riley unclenched her fists and dropped her hands to her sides as she continued. "Your friend Dominique said that you just naturally suspected everybody. So I'm going to take that to mean, like your friend Inspector Moreau, you think I'm in cahoots with whoever is behind this mess."

Jake opened his mouth to respond, but she held up her right hand to stop him as she barreled on. "Nope, don't waste your breath denying it. Despite what you and the good Inspector think, I'm not as dumb as either one of you might think."

"Nobody thinks that you're dumb," Jake sharply cut in.

It was his turn. As she opened her mouth to respond, he cut her off. "I agree with you that we both have a lot at stake here. Your freedom. And my reputation."

Once again she opened her mouth to reply, but he just shook his head at her and kept on talking. "You are wrong about Moreau. And you are definitely wrong about me."

Riley cocked a questioning eyebrow at him.

"I'm willing to admit that I did have my own reasons for bailing you out of jail."

"Bait," Riley declared.

A hint of embarrassment slid across his face as he nodded in agreement. "Blunt, but accurate."

As the banked anger once again started to flare higher in her eyes, he hurried on. "But protection as well."

"Protection?"

A blind man couldn't have missed the sarcasm and skepticism lacing her voice. "In that order," Jake had the decency to admit.

"Fine," Riley said as she once again tried to step around him to get to the door. "But that doesn't change a thing. I still intend to talk to Bill Larson and confront him about drugging me."

When she grabbed the door handle, Jake put his hand down on top hers to keep to her from opening the door, as he continued. "It's too dangerous for you. If you're right about Larson drugging you."

"You know I am," she snapped at him.

Nodding, he continued calmly. "If he did, Moreau will find out and take it from there."

Gritting her teeth and pulling her hand free, Riley glared at Jake. "Moreau doing his job is not my concern. Clearing my name is."

"They are one and the same thing."

Despite her best intentions to keep her temper under control Riley once again found herself angrily shaking her head at him. "Not from where I'm standing, they're not."

As Jake continued to calmly look at her, Riley could feel her temper building up steam. "Moreau might be a good cop like you claim, but he doesn't know Bill Larson like I do." Anger management was all well and good. But just thinking about the creep and what he had done to her stoked her growing anger.

"As far as I'm concerned, the guy is a First Class liar. And the only way I'm going to clear my name is to confront him about the Rohypnol," she said.

"Moreau will do just that."

Riley locked eyes with Jake. "No. This directly concerns me. Nobody drugs me and gets away with it."

"If he did it, he isn't going to get away with it."

"'If?" Riley lost it. Her temper blazed white hot. "There is no 'if he did it'. He did do it. And I'm going to prove it."

Strengthened by her anger Riley shoved Jake away from the door and wrenched it open. Stalking across the foyer she jabbed the elevator call button before turned to look back at him as he followed her out of the open apartment. "Don't even think you are going to stop me."

Jake found himself more amused by the fierce look on her face than he should have been. Holding both hands palms up in mock surrender he took a step back from her.

"Good," she said turning back to face the elevator door. Watching the lights flash as the car rose upward she tried to ignore him standing behind her. She knew without looking that he had a smirk on his face because he thought he had the upper hand. Well let him think that because she knew better.

Like her Dad taught her growing up *'Fool me once, shame on you. Fool me twice, shame on me.'* Mark Scanlon had fooled her once. And he would be the last man to ever do that to her. As Bill Larson was about to find out.

The ding of the opening elevator door broke through her reverie. Ignoring Jake, she stepped determinedly into the car and pushed the button for the ground floor. Turning around, she was glad to see that he hadn't tried to follow her. Giving him a curt nod she glanced towards the still open elevator doors. They seemed to be frozen. Frowning slightly, she punched the ground floor button again as Jake stood silently watching her from the middle of the foyer.

Nothing happened so she then tried the "close door" button.

Again there was no response from the control panel.

Just as she glanced back at the still open elevator doors, a slight smile quirked the corner of Jake's mouth as he held up an electronic key card in his right hand.

"It won't move without this."

Sighing and rolling her eyes at him she gestured to the control panel facing her on the left. "OK, then swipe the card and let me get on my way."

Jake made no move to comply.

"You don't have a clue where to find Larson."

Riley narrowed her eyes at him. "I'll just check with Silvia Longazini. She'll know."

"What makes you so sure of that?"

Annoyed by the delay, Riley threw a quick glance at the top of the elevator car before replying. Giving him a tight smile she said, "Trust me. With Étienne dead, we're now out of a job. So Bill's primary concern will be his paycheck. And that means that he'll check in with Silvia about collecting it."

Jake liked the logic behind her answer. But that didn't mean he was going to cooperate with her and release the elevator for her.

"OK. But how are you going to get to wherever it is he's staying once you find that out? You don't have a car or any money with you."

Glaring across the short distance separating them Riley could feel the muscles in her jaw clenching. His face may have had a neutral expression on it, but Jake's eyes gave him away. She could see the smug amusement dancing in them as he looked at her.

"Not a problem," she said through stiff lips. "I've got two feet. I know how to walk."

"Really?"

Riley ground her teeth and then plastered a forced smile on her face. "Yes, really. I'm actually very good at it. I've had a lot of practice. I've been doing it for years."

Watching her struggle to rein in her temper, Jake had to admit he was finding her determination amusing. If she was still talking to him when this was all over with, he definitely wanted to get to know her better. Not that he was sexually attracted to her.

Yeah, right. Who did he think he was kidding? She was the first woman since Lily who reminded him what it felt like to be a man.

But that was neither here nor there. He had a job to do and he most certainly was not doing it running on about how attractive he was finding Ms. Riley Cooper. So it was back to work, mate.

"I'm glad to hear that. But the elevator is still not going anywhere," he said.

Like a summer lightning strike, a quick flash of anger flickered across Riley's face before she could stop it. Grimacing with determination, she replastered the thin smile back on her face as she stepped out of the elevator car.

Smiling in satisfaction, Jake gestured for her to precede him back into the waiting apartment.

"No thanks," Riley said as she headed towards the fire stair well door she spotted a few yards away.

Realizing her intentions, Jake grabbed her by the arm as she started to move past him. "You'll trigger the fire alarm if you open that door."

Riley looked him in the eye as she jerked her arm free from his grasp. "Tough."

As she started to turn away and continue towards the door, Jake suddenly swooped her off her feet and slung her over his left shoulder.

"What the he...!" Riley yelped as she found herself dangling head down staring at his tight buns. "Put me down this instant!"

Stepping through the open apartment door Jake swung around and used Riley's protruding derriere to push the door closed behind them. Swinging back around, he then marched directly over to the couch and unceremoniously dumped her onto it.

"What do you think you're doing!" she yelled as she struggled to her feet.

Ignoring her, Jake crossed back to the door and engaged its electronic locks. As he turned back to face her, he was startled to find her glaring furiously at him from just inches away.

"Unlock that door this instant!"

"No." Stepping around her he crossed back to the couch and sat down. From over his shoulder he heard Riley angrily rattling the locked door. "It won't open," he called out without turning around.

"You bastard," Riley said stomping back to stand in front of him. "You can't keep me here. That's false imprisonment."

Jake calmly returned her angry glare. "There's nothing false about it."

She looked like she was angry enough to chew through metal spikes, Jake thought amused. She definitely had spunk. He had to give her that.

"You can't hold me here against my will," Riley said quickly scanning the room for a phone.

There wasn't one.

But there was a balcony. And growing up a tomboy did have its advantages. Especially when it came to climbing tall trees – and high rise balconies.

She didn't honestly expect that she could actually make it all the way to the ground floor before Jake and his people caught up with her. But the sight of her dangling from one of the balconies would surely catch somebody's eye. And that attention would be all she needed to help her get away.

"I was rather hoping you would see yourself as a guest and not a prisoner," Jake said as she suddenly glanced over at him with a preoccupied look on her face.

"What?"

Before he could reply, she threw a quick glance over at the kitchen door on the far side of the room. "I'm finding this whole situation a little bit overwhelming. So would you mind terribly getting me a glass of water?"

Instantly getting to his feet Jake peered closely at her face.

Giving him a weak flash of a smile Riley continued, "It's been pretty rough the past few days. And I think it's finally catching up with me." Sinking into the couch across from him she leaned her head against the back rest and closed her eyes.

"Of course. Can I get you anything else?"

She gave him a weak head shake as she continued to rest with her eyes closed.

Turning away, Jake headed for the kitchen. With his back to her he didn't realize that she was watching him through half closed eyelids. The second he disappeared through the kitchen door she was up like a shot and across to the sliding glass door leading out to the balcony.

Throwing a quick look over her shoulder to the kitchen door to confirm that Jake was still out of sight, Riley quickly slid the large glass panel open and bolted to the edge of balcony.

Darting a quick glance over the bronze filigree scrollwork encasing the hanging balcony, her breath caught in her throat when she saw the distance between the floors. Straightening up and sucking in a deep breath, Riley admonished herself. You can do this. You have to do this. Because if you don't, you can definitely forget about breathing fresh air for a very long time

From the kitchen she heard a hidden phone give an abbreviated ring.

"Right," she said to a passing gull riding an invisible air current circling about her.

Throwing a final quick glance over her shoulder, she spotted Jake just as he charged into view from the kitchen door. Their eyes locked in mutual determination

His muffled roar of protest barely registered in her mind as she flung her legs over the grillwork and started to lower herself to the bottom of the balcony.

"Oh no, you don't!" Jake growled into her ear as he leaned over and clamped her left arm in a vise grip.

"Are you out of your bloody mind, woman!" he bellowed yanking her upward and swinging her back onto the balcony.

Shaking her like a rag doll he continued to thunder at her. "You could have killed yourself pulling a stunt like that."

CHAPTER 11

"You are the most reckless woman I have ever dealt with," Jake hissed between clenched teeth as he forced Riley back inside the apartment and flipped the lock on the glass slider.

"I'm not reckless," Riley snapped at him as he turned towards her, "I'm determined."

Glaring at him she continued. "Nobody has a bigger stake in clearing my name than I do. And I can't do that locked up in this place."

Just then the front door suddenly burst open and Max came charging into the room with Apollo dead on his heel. Jake barely glanced at them as Derrick stepped into view behind them.

Whipping his head back towards the glowering Riley, he glared back at her. "Clearing your name isn't going to do you any good if you're dead."

As his three teammates reached them, Jake shook his head at Derrick. "Can you believe that move?"

"Impressive," Derrick said as he dipped his head at Riley. "But completely foolhardy."

As Jake turned to look over at his men, Riley spotted the ear bud he was wearing. So that's how he knew, she thought as she instantly shifted her anger towards Derrick, "Thanks for nothing."

As Derrick gave her a 'what can I say?' shrug, Max broke out into a big grin. "Smooth move. You would have made one heck of a Ranger."

"That or an acrobat," Apollo added as Riley continued to glare at Jake like an enraged bull facing a waving red flag.

"Is anybody interested in what we found out about Bill Larson?" Claudine asked as she walked into the room holding up a silver thumb drive for all to see.

"Larson?" Riley said tearing her eyes away from Jake to look over at the approaching woman. Snapping a quick glance over her shoulder at Jake and the others, she found him warily following her movement as she moved to join Claudine. As she closed the distance, a relaxed Derrick moved to stand next to Jake while both Max and Apollo grabbed themselves a seat on the nearby couches.

"You were checking him out already?"

"Sure. Jake doesn't trust him any more than you do," the Frenchwoman says as she crossed over to an open laptop sitting on a nearby chrome and glass desk.

Reaching the desk, Claudine paused to glance over at Jake as Riley joined her at the desk. "May I?" she asked Jake as she gestured towards the computer.

Giving her a slight shrug he said, "Be my guest."

Giving Riley a hint of a wink, Claudine quickly inserted the thumb drive into the computer's side port as she was taking her seat at the desk. With lightening fast key strokes, she instantly filled the computer screen with a series of overlapping data and photo graphics featuring Bill Larson.

Claudine addressed Jake over the top of her computer screen as he silently joined Riley at the desk. As he reached them, she angled the computer so all three of them could see the screen together. "We re-ran our check on him, but there were no significant changes from our last check."

"But there was a change?" Riley said.

Claudine gave her the merest hint of a shrug as she replied, "Just a couple of long distance phone arguments with his ex-wife who is not happy about him making his child support payments in the middle of the month, instead of at the beginning like she's been demanding since their divorce."

"But he is making the payments, right?" Jake asked.

"Right," Claudine answered.

"And the alibi he gave the police checks out," Derrick said as he joined them at the desk. The building's security monitors picked him up leaving like he told the police."

"Do you have any idea where he went?" Riley asked ignoring Jake as she looked over Derrick.

"The Casino," Claudine answered as she key stroked in a security video feed from the Monte Carlo Casino lobby. "Recognize anyone?" she asked Riley as a lanky blond with thinning collar length hair crossed the opulent casino lobby and approached a curvaceous brunette in a skin-tight emerald satin sheath dress. The woman was sipping from a champagne glass and casually glancing around the crowded lobby when the blond approached and said something to her in greeting.

"That's Bill Larson," Riley said as she watched the screen. "Is there any audio?"

"Unfortunately, no," Derrick answered for Claudine as he moved closer to the desk so that he had a fuller view of the laptop's monitor.

In his brown sports jacket and tan slacks Larson stood out from the surrounding tuxedoed and bejeweled crowd swirling around him and the brunette. Riley watched as the woman deftly deposited her half empty champagne glass on a passing waiter's tray and slipped her arm through Bill's as she smiled and gave him her full attention.

"I don't understand," Riley said glancing up at Jake and the others as Apollo and Max joined the group to watch the video.

"Neither do I," said Apollo as Larson and the woman headed for the exit. "That guy's a total loser."

"But he ends up with her," Max completed his friend's sentence as they both shook their heads at the sight of Larson and his date disappearing through the casino's front door.

"No," Riley said with a slight shake her head. "What I don't understand is what he's doing there in the first place?

"People like Bill and I might work here in Monaco," she continued. "But we don't make the kind of money it takes to hang out with millionaires. Those folks are from a completely different paddock."

"Her name is Gabrielle LeFleuer. Do you know her?" Jake asked Riley.

"No," Riley answered shaking her head. "But she looks expensive."

Jake stares at her. "How do you know that?"

Riley pointed to the monitor where Claudine had frozen the video on the shot of Bill and his female companion as they approached the casino's front doors on their way out of the lobby. "Look at that diamond encrusted wrist watch she's wearing."

"Do you know what she is" Derrick said

"I'm presuming she's a call girl," Riley answered.

102

"A very, very expensive call girl," Apollo added.

"'Escort.' Gentlemen." Claudine said grinning over the top of her monitor at Apollo and Max.

"An 'escort' who makes $50K for one night's work," Max added.

"Fifty thousand dollars!" Riley said glancing over at Max who nodded back in silent reply. "For one night?"

"Yep," Max said grinning at her.

"'Escort' or call girl, it doesn't make any difference," Riley said. "Whatever she is, she's definitely out of Bill Larson's price range."

"How can you tell," Jake asked. "Aside from Max here telling you her going rate?"

Riley looked over at him. "Her wrist watch costs more than Bill's entire annual salary."

"She's got a good eye," Derrick said quietly into Jake's ear as Riley continued.

"Bill's got a real bad gambling problem," Riley said ignoring Derrick's comment. "This is the best paying job he's ever had. But as good as the pay is, it's definitely not good enough that he can afford to hang out at the Monte Carlo Casino."

"Or afford the services of his 'date'," Max muttered to his buddy Apollo.

"My point exactly," Riley agreed with him.

"And that's why I want you," Jake said to his team as he closed the lid on the laptop, "to find out who was picking up her tab that night."

"You don't think it was Larson?" Derrick asked.

"Not unless Gabrielle was doing charity work that night."

"Right," Max laughed. "A hooker with a heart of gold."

"'Escort.' Max," Apollo grinned at him. "Remember the lady isn't a 'hooker' she's an 'escort'."

"What's the difference?"

"About fifty thousand dollar a customer," Riley said drolly.

"Good one, Riley," Claudine laughed.

Jake cut them off by turning to Derrick. "Find out who picked up her tab that night."

Derrick gave him a curt nod in response as he continued. "And if it turns out that Larson did, I want to know where he got the money from to do it."

"Got it," Derrick replied. "Meanwhile, what are you going to be doing?"

Jake glanced over at Riley as he answered. "We're going to have a little talk, in person, with Mr. Larson."

"About what?" Claudine asked as Jake started for the door with Riley at his side.

"A tube of toothpaste," a grinning Riley threw back over her shoulder as she stepped through the front door Jake was holding open for her. As the two of them disappeared through the open door, Claudine and the others exchanged bewildered looks.

"Toothpaste?" Max said.

"Don't ask," Claudine cut him off as she fired up the laptop to begin trolling for information.

CHAPTER 12

Jake turned up the sharply inclined street leading into the narrow canyon tucked into one of the many folds of the hills encircling Monaco. Unlike the grand boulevards lining the harbor areas, this humble street was narrow and snaked up the side of the scrub-covered hillside as it wound its way up towards the crest of the hill. Tidy, sun-drenched houses lined the down slope side of the street. Pomegranate and olive trees shaded tiny courtyards and empty driveways.

The dry Mediterranean heat wafted in through their open windows along with the chirps and twitters of the birds flitting among the scrubs and low laying trees covering the surrounding hillsides. Riley could feel the warm breezes gently drying the sheen of perspiration on the back of her neck. And she could smell faint traces of an unknown spice on the welcome breezes swirling into the sun baked car.

"Where exactly are we going," she said as Jake guided the car around a small delivery van half filling the road outside of a *boulangerie-pâtisserie* shop swarming with mid-morning customers.

"Larson is camping out with the Devereuxes' chauffeur Maurice," he said as he eased their car back into its lane and continued up the hill. "Devereux owns a little *pied-à-terre* up here where he stores a few of his extra cars."

Jake threw her a quick glance before returning his attention to the winding road ahead. "Maurice lives in the apartment over the garage."

Just as she started to nod in response Jake broke out into a grin at the sight of an open parking space along the crowded street. "We're in luck."

Zipping into the space just as the car behind them suddenly gunned its engine and went roaring past, Jake shut off the engine. Then he leaned back in his seat so she could have a better view of the building across the street from them.

"There it is," he said as she leaned forward to look out his driver's side window.

Riley took in the view of the white-washed stucco and timbered two car garage with its gabled loft apartment. Cascades of bright red geraniums filled the hunter green window boxes lining the four double paned windows overlooking the street below. A glass-paned Dutch door was tucked into the downhill side of the building at street level.

"Are you sure Bill's in there?"

Jake glanced over at the apartment as he answered her. "This is where he's living at the moment." He turned back to look at her as he continued. "If he's not there at the moment, I'll let Apollo and Max know."

Opening his driver's side door Jake climbed out from behind the wheel and Riley followed his lead. As she was closing her door, Jake turned back to look over the roof of the car at her. "Then they can keep an eye on the place and let us know when he returns."

"Okay," she said as she came around the front end of the car and joined him.

Waiting together to allow an approaching car to move pass them, Riley was aware of the comforting sense of security Jake's presence gave her in the midst of the chaos that her life had suddenly become. Not that she'd ever admit that to him of course. But she did appreciate it even if she'd never actually tell him that. Especially since they really weren't work colleagues given their different positions within the Devereux household.

But it was nice to know he was around. Even if he was using her for bait. And who was she to complain about that since she was using him as well.

As soon as the car was out of their way, Jake placed his hand lightly on the small of her back to guide her across the street. To her surprise the light touch of his fingers on her lower back unexpectedly sent a tingling feeling radiating out through her whole body. The sudden rush of the feeling caused her breath to catch slightly as she hurried across the sunny street towards the door leading up to the window-lined loft apartment.

Reaching the door, Jake push the door bell button next to the right door jamb. As he did Riley stepped away from the building in order to look up at the curtained windows overlooking the street. She was hoping to catch sight of Bill checking out the window when he responded to the door bell. But there was no sign of any movement at all from the apartment.

"Anything?" Jake asked as he stabbed the door bell three more times with no sounds of movement at all from the other side of the door.

"Nothing," Riley said as she returned to his side. "I guess he's not home after all. Maybe we should have called first."

"No," Jake said shaking his head. "That's not a good idea."

"Why not?"

"Because that gives him time to take off," Jake said looking at her. "Or time to get his story together for us when we got here."

On a whim Jake reached out and tried the door knob. "This way he doesn't have time to prepare his answers."

"But he wouldn't know what you were going to ask him," Riley said as the knob turned in Jake's hand.

That was not what Jake was expecting. But it was what he had hoped for.

Glancing over at Riley he held a warning finger up to his lips. "Stay down here," he said softly. "And I'll check it out."

"Forget it," Riley said in a normal tone of voice. "I'm coming with you."

"You don't know what we'll find up there," he said.

"Neither do you," she replied firmly.

Jake threw a quick look at the door he had opened just enough for the door lock to clear the wooden jamb. "I don't like this," he said as he held the door in place. "We could be walking into a trap."

"Nobody knew we were coming."

Jake shook his head in response. "That doesn't mean anything. If something's wrong, whoever caused it could have still set a trap to cover his tracks and delay pursuit."

"Well we won't know for sure just standing around down here," Riley said in a fierce whisper. "Will we?"

Rolling his eyes and shaking his head slightly at her stubborn determination to make his life more complicated than it already was, Jake scowled back at her. "Make sure you stay behind me."

"Do I look stupid to you?"

When he glanced back at her, she immediately cocked her head at him. "That was rhetorical."

"Right," he said with a final shake of his head.

Glancing up and down the street to ensure that no one was watching them, Jake held onto the door knob with his left hand while he used his right to unsnap his shoulder holster and ease his gun out. Riley licked her suddenly dry lips at the sight of his Sig Sauer held at his beltline inside his open jacket.

Throwing her a quick nod, Jake turned away and silently eased the curtain windowed door open. It swung wide to reveal a wooden staircase leading up to a small landing fronting a plain wooden door.

Stepping into the tiny foyer at the base of the stairs, Jake motioned for Riley to stay against the shadowed wall to his left as he started up the stairs. Shaking her head in refusal, she stayed on his heels as she followed him up the stairs to the small landing above.

Reaching the top step, Jake motioned for Riley to halt on the step below him where she would be out of any line of fire. When she started to refuse, he moved away from the wall so that she could see what he had already discovered – the door to the apartment was not fully closed. Through the open crack they could see morning sunlight streaming into the apartment from the windows lining the rear of the building. This time when Jake threw her a look, Riley meekly backed down a couple of steps to give him room to work.

Stepping onto the landing, Jake silently darted to the left of the door. Shielded by the wall he used the tip of his gun to slowly inch the door open wide enough for him to begin scanning the room for any sign of an intruder. When the door was half opened, he gave it a quick shove and dived through the opening. Shoulder rolling to his left he was up in a crouch and clearing the room in the blink of an eye.

As the tip of his gun swept a 300° arc, Jake was greeted only by the stifling silence of the room. A quick glance was all he needed to take in the faded couch and two cushioned armchairs and large flat screen TV that filled the main room's center area.

Silent as a sparrow he glided across the room to the nearest open doorway that led into a tiny, sun-filled utilitarian kitchen. Aside from the chipped metal table with two companion chairs, and the usual kitchen appliances, it was empty.

Moving swiftly to the next open doorway he found a second empty room. It was an unadorned bedroom containing a set of sagging twin beds and a plain wooden five-drawer dresser and a single wooden nightstand separating the two beds. Piles of clothes in a corner next to one bed barely registered in his mind's eyes as he immediately swung around and headed for the last of the three open doorways lining the main living room area. That turned out to be a small empty bathroom. Two separate shaving kits cluttered the top of the sink counter and a damp bath towel was draped haphazardly over the aluminum shower rod.

Swinging around from the open bathroom door Jake found Riley standing in front of the center living room window staring down at something lying on the floor at her feet. As he started to cross over to her, she looked up at him with a grim look on her face.

Coming around the edge of the couch he caught sight of Bill Larson face down on the hardwood floor. A wide circle of coppery-smelling blood pooled around his head. Moving closer to the body Jake noted that the dead man's ankles were twisted around each other like vines.

Riley indicated the scorch marks and hole in the material two feet above the center point of the white lace curtains "It was a clean head shot," she said as Jake reached her side. "He was dead before he hit the floor."

Jake was already scanning the angle of trajectory through the window in order to find the sniper's firing position. It was in the cluster of bushes about ten feet above where he was currently parked.

"Are you okay?" Jake said as he continued to scan the hillside through the scrim of lacey material covering the window.

"I'm mad," Riley said in reply.

That earned her a quick glance before Jake returned his eyes to the window in front of him. "Mad?"

"Yes!" Riley said as she moved to the opposite end of the body in order to look at the twisted ankles. "There goes my only chance of clearing my name."

'Jacketed round' Jake thought when he spotted the small hole in the window glass. Turning around his eyes scanned the back wall for the missing bullet. He didn't find anything until he looked down at what was left of Larson's head. Frangible bullet. Military issue.

Now that's definitely odd he thought as he glanced up at Riley standing near Larson's feet.

"He was facing the window when he caught the round," she said.

"Yep," Jake replied as he holstered his gun and joined her. "The impact spun him around."

"Thus the twisted ankles," she said looking across the body at him.

He nodded at her.

"Frangible bullet, metal jacked, military issue," she continued.

Catching sight of his arched eyebrow she gave him a half shrug. "Three tours in a combat zone really expands a girl's repertoire of small talk."

Sighing in disappointment, Riley turned to head to the phone sitting on a small round table near the open door. "The way my luck is going," she said over her shoulder to Jake, "I expect your friend Inspector Moreau is going to be charging me with this murder as well."

"What are you doing?" Jake asked.

Riley paused to turn back towards him. "We have to call the police."

At that instance, a flock of birds exploded from the cluster of bushes on the hillside above his car.

"NO!" Jake roared as he launched himself at a stunned Riley.

Just as he tackled her at her waist, the living room window glass imploded and the lace curtains shredded as a 6" metal rocket flew into the room.

Riley barely had time to register the pain from Jake slamming into her. Just as she started to fold like a collapsing brick wall, the entire room erupted into a massive fireball of flames, flying metal shrapnel, razor-sharp wooden splinters. At the same instant, the stench of roasted flesh, and the smell of burning wool and spent cordite, filled her nose and mouth.

CHAPTER 13

Like an erupting geyser the force of the blast hurled Jake and Riley through the open apartment door and smashed them against the wooden landing railing. The railing splintered under their combined weight, and they plummeted over the edge, as belching flames licked the open doorway behind them. Tumbling in mid-air Jake twisted his body under Riley's in order to cushion her just as they slammed into the floor near the base of the stairs.

The impact drove all of the air from Riley's lungs and she had no strengthen in her body to draw any back in. She felt as if she was being crushed by the weight of the entire world sitting on her chest. Growing black spots were rapidly eclipsing the distant blinding light around her. And the tinny ringing of a roaring waterfall was telescoping away from her.

"Breathe," she heard someone yelling from across a distance as wide as the Grand Canyon. But it couldn't be talking to her because the world was crushing her as flat as an autumn leaf.

Just as the spiraling blackness was rushing forward to engulf her, and pull her into its stygian depths, a hurricane force wind was jammed down her spasming throat and into her flattened lungs. With an explosive pop that rang in her ears, both of her lungs suddenly re-inflated. And a storm of fresh, sweet air rushed in to push back the encroaching blackness that had been engulfing her. As the blackness retreated, the glare of the fire raging over her head almost blinded her with its intensity.

Lifting his mouth from hers, Jake shouted into her face. ""Riley! Can you hear me?"

Weakly she rolled her eyes in the direction of his voice.

"Breathe," he told her. "Keep taking deep breaths. You just had the wind knocked out of you."

Feebly nodding her head in response, she pulled in as much air as she could swallow before Nature took over and steadied her breath back to normal.

She felt as weak as a newborn kitten laying there at the foot of the stairs. Every bone and muscle in her body throbbed with a firestorm of sparking pains. But she was alive and that's all that mattered at the moment.

"Thank you," she whispered as she rolled her head towards Jake, who had slumped back against the nearby newel post. "Let's not do that again, anytime soon."

"You've got my vote on that," he said just as a spasm of pain contorted his face and he hunched forward to clutch his blood soaked left shoulder.

The sight of Jake's wounded shoulder acted like a shot of adrenaline to Riley's system. Instantly all of her own aches and pains receded into the background as she lasered in on the wounded man next to her. Rolling over onto her stomach she shakily got to her knees and shuffled to his side.

"You're hurt," she said as she reached to pull his bloodied hand away so she could examine his injury.

As she reached towards him, Jake grabbed her wrist to stop her. "First things first," he said. "We've got something more important to thank about at the moment," he continued as he jerked his head in the direction of the fire raging over their heads in the apartment above.

Leaning forward in order to get to his feet he told her, "The first thing we need to do is get out of here."

As he leaned forward, Riley caught sight of the jagged shard of wood protruding from his shoulder blade. The piece she could see was more than a foot long.

"Jake!" she said as she grabbed him to keep him from toppled face down onto the foyer floor. "You can't go anywhere with that sticking out of you like that."

His lips white with pain Jake shook his head at her as he said through clenched teeth. "That fire is not going to wait for that. You can take care of it once we're out of here."

Riley was about to argue with him when a sudden explosion rocked the entire building and a massive fireball belched through the open doorway above them. The explosion sent a shower of fiery debris raining down on their heads. Instinctively they both ducked and covered their heads as best they could against the shower of sparks and debris pouring down on them.

"Looks like the fire has found the kitchen gas line," Jake said.

The instant the firestorm began to lighten up Riley was on her feet and dragging Jake to his.

"You're right. We definitely have to get out of here, now!" she said as they staggered the few feet to the entry door.

With Jake leaning heavily on her left shoulder Riley reached out and pulled open the door leading out to the street. And just as she did, a high powered rifle round slammed into the door just inches from her head. As the bullet sent splinters of wood flying in all directions, Jake instinctively yanked her into the shelter of the foyer.

"What…?" Riley yelped as they stumbled back from the open door and the beckoning safety of the sun drenched street beyond.

"Our sniper friend is obviously still out there." Jake said as he clenched his lips against the fiery pain that was threatening to take him down any minute now.

Reaching into his jacket pocket Jake pulled out his cell phone and hit the speed dial button. Holding the phone up to his ear he listened for a second and then frowned at the phone.

"What's the matter?" Riley asked as he snapped it shut and shoved it back into his trouser pocket.

"It's broke," he said. "I must have landed on it when we fell."

Through the open door they both caught the faintest hint of a police siren off in the far distance.

"The police," Riley said with relief. "Now we'll be safe."

Jake shook his head at her as she continued to support his heavier weight on her shoulder. "Don't count on it."

He indicated the flames that continued to rage overhead. "By the time they get here that will have killed us if we don't get out of here."

Riley looked towards the nearby open door. "And if we try to go out there, the sniper will kill us."

"Interesting situation," Jake said in an attempt at humor. "Don't you think."

Glancing at him Riley suddenly caught sight of his holstered gun under his jacket and suddenly broke out into a smile.

"I've got an idea," she said as she began to lead Jake over to the bottom steps of the stairs.

Helping him to ease down on the step she said, "We need to get your jacket off."

Puzzled Jake silently nodded in response.

"I'm sorry, but it's going to hurt," she said as she began to slip his uninjured arm out of the sleeve.

"Is it going to help get us out of here?"

Riley nodded at him as pulled the jacket free from his right side.

"Then I can live with a little pain," he said looking her in the eyes. "Do what you have to do."

Giving him a curt nod she took a deep breath and then let it out. "Right," she said

Moving behind Jake so that she had more room to work, Riley grabbed the jacket material around the knife-like shard of wood still protruding from his back. Taking a deep breath to steady her hands she gave the material a sudden jerk in order to widen the hole around the splinter. As she did, a muffled grunt of pain escaped Jake's lips before he could seal them tight against any further sounds.

"Sorry," she murmured to his broad back.

Wetting her parched lips Riley once again grabbed the torn jacket material near the bottom of the tear and gave it a second jerk to widen the tear even further. This time Jake was a silent as a stone.

Satisfied with the results, Riley then gently worked the jacket free from the protrusion and moved around to Jake's left side. There she slipped the jacket free from his blood soaked left arm as he cradled it with his uninjured right hand.

"Okay, the hard part's over," she said looking at the sheen covering his pain filled faced.

"Now what?" Jake croaked from his tight throat. Clearing his throat he continued in a more normal voice. "What do you need me to do?"

Riley gave him a tight smile. "I need two things from you."

He nodded for her to go on.

"First, I'll need your gun."

He arched both eyebrows at her before freeing his gun from its holster and holding it out to her.

"Thanks. Can you hold onto it for a moment while I take care of the jacket?"

"I'm not going anywhere." He said giving her a flash of a smile.

Turning away from him, Riley scanned the piles of debris littering the small foyer. Kicking aside scrapes scattered around she quickly found what she needed – a baluster broken free from the landing railing when they crashed through it earlier. Taking an extra couple of seconds she moved into the shadows filling the back of the small foyer area.

"What are you looking for?"

Stepping back into his line of sight she said, "Found it."

Returning back to Jake she hooked his torn jacket over the end of the baluster. "If you sit over next to the door jamb, do you think you can dangle this so that the sniper can see it?"

"Yes," Jake said cautiously. "And while I'm doing that what are you going to be doing?"

Before she can answer him Jake holds his gun up between them. "Because if you're thinking of using this to take him out, it's not going to happen. It doesn't have the range you'd need."

"I was going to give it a try, she said as a smile tugged at the corners of her lips. "But now I don't have to."

"Meaning?"

"Meaning," Riley said, "we're in luck."

She jerked her head in the direction of the rear of the foyer. "There's a locked door at the back that we can use to get out of here."

"Great," Jake said. "Then let's go."

"It's locked so we'll need to shoot out the lock."

Jake nods at her.

"And when our friend out there hears that, he's going to come running and hunt us down before we can get away."

"OK, but at least we'll be away from the fire."

"You're in no condition to travel fast. So I need to get us out of here. And keep our friend pinned down long enough for you to get safely away."

"I'm not leaving you here." Jake insisted.

"Don't worry about me," Riley said with a shake of her head. "I've been hunting wild animals since I was a kid. I can take care of myself."

"That's not a wild animal out there," Jake said glaring at her. "Whoever he is, he's trained. And he damn good at killing his targets."

"He didn't kill us," Riley said quietly.

"Yet," Jake countered.

"That's why we've got to get out of here without him realizing we're gone."

Jake shook his head at her. "Like you said, he'll hear you when you shoot out the lock and figure that we're ducking out the back way."

"Not if I do it under cover of his own gunfire."

Jake looked at the jacket she held dangling on the end of the pole. By the tiny nodding of his head as he figured out what she had in mind Riley could tell he thought that her game plan just might work.

"OK," he finally said. "But only under one condition. We go out that back door together and down the canyon together."

"Absolutely," Riley said firmly.

Jake gave her a piercing look before finally nodding in agreement. "OK," he said. "Let's move out."

Grinning at him, Riley helped Jake to move over next to the partially opened door and handed him the decoy jacket. "Are you sure you're going to be OK," she asked, as perspiration sheened his upper lips.

"Fine. Now let's just do it," Jake said holding the gun out to her.

Giving him a sharp nod, Riley took the offered gun and hurried towards the back of the foyer. From the shadows she called out to him. "Go!"

Leaning heavily against the wall, Jake dangled the bloodied jacket in the open doorway. That triggered an instant response from the sniper who fired a single round that tore through the already bloodied sleeve before Jake could yank it back out of view.

"Riley?" he called out.

"Sorry, one more time. I wasn't quite ready."

Again Jake edged the decoy into view. Only this time he heard what the sniper couldn't as his round drilled through the wood of the front door – the sound of Riley shooting off the back door lock. As he turned to look in her direction, the back door swung open and bright daylight poured into the shattered room.

Hurrying back to his side a grinning Riley said, "I hope that you're not waiting for an engraved invitation to get the heck out of this place."

Holding up his gun for him to see, she tucked it into waistband of her jeans. "I'm going to hold onto this for now. In case we run into more trouble."

Swaying on his feet Jake knew he was in no position to argue with her. Especially since she could clearly handle herself in a tight situation. "OK," he said as she came towards him.

Wrapping Jake's good arm around her shoulders, Riley hurried him out the back door and towards the door she spotted at the back of the privacy fence as they stepped outside. As they stumble towards the fence, the wailing of approaching police and fire sirens began to fill the air around them and they spotted frightened neighbors in the surrounding houses peeking through curtained windows.

"I don't know about you, but I really don't want to get tied up for the next couple of days at the police station," Jake said as they slipped through the fence door and out of sight of the burning building.

"You'll definitely get no argument from me," Riley said. "If I never see the inside of another police station again, it will be too soon for me."

Looking around them Riley realized that they were standing on the terraced uphill side of the down slope neighbor's yard. Seeing the steps cut into the hill that led down to the front of the property and the road beyond Riley let out a sigh of relief.

Turning to Jake she said, "Can you make it down to the road?"

But before he could answer her, a black-gloved hand clamped over her mouth from behind.

CHAPTER 14

"Don't scream," a man's voice whispered into her ear.

Riley moved before she even had time to think. The forearm clamping her tight against a set of rock hard abs was as thick as an mountain oak branch. She could smell mint on his breath and the hint of citrus aftershave as his cheek brushed against the side of her face.

As those sensory impressions flashed through her mind, her muscles acted with a will of their own. Lifting her right leg knee high she scraped along the inside of his shin bone as she slammed her foot down on the middle of the arch of his foot. At the same time she slammed the back of her skull into the center of his nose.

His reaction was instantaneous and almost — but not quite - as expected.

His head flew back and his body bowed as he expelled a muffled grunt of pain. But she had to give him credit for still maintaining his grip on her. Others would have been reaching for their nose which was spewing blood like a broken water main.

He managed to keep his grip on her, but it had loosen just enough for her to be able to grab the thumb covering her mouth and bend it straight back until it touched his wrist. At the same time she ducked and twisted and, using his arm as a lever, she used his own weight to flip him over her hip and send him flying over her head to land flat on his back next to Jake's feet.

"Apollo how many times have I told you not to sneak up on a girl like that," Riley heard Claudine Reynard laugh as she stepped into her line of sight. Despite the mild weather, she was wearing a summer short sleeved jacket over her V necked T-shirt and jeans. Giving Riley a friendly smile she holstered her 9 mm behind her back as she crossed over to Apollo and Jake.

"I unk uhe oke my ose," the blond sprawled at Jake's feet complained from behind the hand cupping the middle of his face.

"Serves you right for being so careless," Jake said as he gave Riley a conspiratorial wink.

"Apollo," Riley said hurrying over to the fallen man. "I'm so sorry."

"Don't be," Claudine told her as she held out her hand to pull her fallen companion to his feet. "Jake's right, he shouldn't have been so careless."

As Apollo sat up, Riley could see the blood cascading from his twisted nose. "Put your head back. It'll help stop the bleeding."

Claudine took in the sight of Jake's bloody arm then turned to Riley. "Your handiwork too?"

Jake turned slightly so both Claudine and Apollo caught sight of the jagged splinter of wood piercing his shoulder. "Not this time."

"Ouch, boss," Apollo said as he got to his feet. "Looks like you got the bigger 'owie' award this time. We need to get you to a hospital and have them take care of that," Apollo said as he moved around to Jake's good side so he could help him down the hillside.

"No," Jake said shaking his head at Apollo. "We can't take a chance of Moreau finding out and then tying us up with questions right now."

Jake looked over at Riley. "Can you handle it?"

"Do I have any choice?"

"You always have choices," he said.

Choices, Riley thought. Right. She had the choice to marry a thief and liar. She had the choice to find herself accused of killing two people she considered the closest to being a friend that she had had in a long, long time. Then she had the choice of having a complete stranger try to blow her to smithereens with an anti-tank rocket.

Yep, she had a lot of choices all right. And none of them had been her own. And where had they gotten her?

Certainly not where she thought she was going to be, that was for sure.

Well she definitely had a choice right now.

She could run or she could fight and take back control of her life instead of letting other people dictate what her life was going to be. She didn't ask for this mess, but she was in it whether she liked it or not.

If circumstances had been different, Riley knew what she would have chosen. But that was before and this was now.

So what was she going to do about it?

Make a choice....

Returning Jake's gaze, she gave him the barest of nods.

A look of satisfaction filled his eyes as he then turned to the waiting Apollo, "You ready?"

When Apollo nodded reluctantly in agreement, Riley threw a concerned glance up the hill towards the burning building. "We need to get out of here now. There's a sniper up there somewhere looking for us," she said.

"Not a problem," Apollo told her as he and Jake started down the steps.

"Derrick and Max went hunting for him," Claudine said as the two men moved past her to start down the neighbor's garden steps. "But he managed to slip away before they could get close enough to tag him."

Keeping her eyes on the fence encircling the Devereux property she gestured for Riley to go ahead of her down the slope.

Jake called over his shoulder to her, "I left the car parked across the street from the place."

"Yeah we saw it when we drove up," Apollo said from behind the hand cupping his injured nose. "Max grabbed it already."

Apollo gestured towards the street below them. "He and Derrick should be waiting for us down there."

"How did you know we needed help?" Riley said keeping a watchful eye on both men as they moved down the steps and across the neighbor's backyard, heading for the gate at the side of the house.

"Police band radio," Claudine said as she and Riley hurried to catch up with their two companions. Behind them they all could hear the commotion of the firemen attacking the blaze shooting out of the roof of Devereux's building.

Claudine moved to the front of the group to go through the gate first. "When we heard the report of the fire at Devereux's garage, we figured that you two might need some backup."

As Jake nodded his approval at her, Claudine slipped through the gate and moved to the front of the house to check the street in both directions. Pulling a set of car keys out of her back pocket she called over her shoulder to the others. "OK, it's all clear."

Moving swiftly she crossed the lawn to the black SUV parked at the curb. As she moved, she keyed open the locks and opened both passenger side doors so that her three companions could move directly into the waiting vehicle. As they did, she kept a watchful eye on the empty street for any signs of trouble.

Apollo helped Jake into the back seat and then stepped aside and motioned for Riley to join him there. Moving past him she gave him a grateful nod.

As Riley was climbing into the car, Claudine hurried around the front of the vehicle and jumped behind the wheel. The moment Riley was inside, Apollo slammed the door closed behind her and eased into the front seat. Before he could even pull his door closed Claudine was already pulling away from the curb and heading down the street towards the flatland below. As they sped away from the house, a second black SUV and Jake's car peeled away from the curb and fell into formation behind them.

Glancing into her rear view mirror Claudine spotted a worried Riley peering nervously out their rear window. "It's OK. It's just Derrick and Max."

As relief filled her face, Riley gave her a quick nod. Then she turned her full attention to dealing with Jake's injury.

CHAPTER 15

"Will you please slow down," Riley said to Jake as he hurried along the long, cream-colored corridor.

"I've got things to do."

"What you should be doing," she said, "is resting. I just put 120 stitches into that shoulder. And you could tear them loose flailing around."

"Flailing?" Jake said scowling over his shoulder at her. "How in the world could I possibly flail anything? You've got my arm bound up tighter than a Christmas goose."

Reaching a T-intersection Jake turned right and headed for the door at the end of this short section of the corridor.

"You need to be in bed resting," Riley insisted as they reached the closed door with its electronic keypad.

The merest hint of a smile tugged at the corner of Jake's mouth as he keyed in the entry code. "Are you offering to keep me company, by any chance?"

As the lock released, Jake caught the look of surprise on Riley's face. Opening the door and gesturing for her to enter he said, "That was a bad attempt at humor."

"Right," she said as she stepped through the open door. "I knew that."

As Riley moved into the room in front of them, Jake mentally kicked himself. What in the world were you thinking with that bloody schoolboy crack, he chided himself. You're lucky she didn't break *your* nose with that remark.

Bullet resistant glass lined the far wall and revealed a balcony that appeared to be set back into the face of the cliff overlooking the entrance to Monaco's old harbor. Between the door and the glass wall the center of the room with filled with six individual computerized workstations with built-in monitors and keyboards.

Raised platform walkways lined the entire length of walls on either side of the room from where Jake and Riley were standing. The platforms enclosed a recessed work pit filled with individualized computer ladened workstations

A brushed chromed safety handrail, interrupted in the middle for access, lined the length of both platforms. On the platforms themselves floor to ceiling computers, wall-mounted monitor screens and banks of flashing electronic servers filled every inch of wall space.

"What is this?" Riley asked as her eyes swept across the panorama of wall mounted computer monitors and workstations straight out of NASA's Houston control center. Turning to look back at Jake as he closed the door behind him she said, "This looks like the bridge of the Enterprise."

"I loved Star Trek," Max said looking up from computer screen at the workstation he was standing next to in the pit. Seated in front of the console was a raccoon-eyed Apollo sporting a large white bandage across the bridge of his nose. Looking over the top of his eye-level console he gave Riley a friendly wink as he paused in his task.

On the platform to their left Derrick left Claudine reviewing the sheaf of pages she was holding while he came down to greet them. Warily eying the sling holding Jake's arm tight across his chest. "How's the shoulder?"

"I'll live," Jake answered as Claudine laid her stack of papers on the console she was standing next to, and followed Derrick off the platform to greet them.

"Looks like you did a great job," she said smiling at Riley.

Claudine couldn't help noticing the drawn look around Riley's eyes. Jerking her thumb in Apollo's direction she continued. "These two are doing just fine. The question is, how are you doing?"

"I'll be OK," Riley said returning her smile with a weaker image of her own.

Riley turned her head to take in the entire room. "Is this where you normally work?"

"Some of the time," Jake answered for the others as he moved deeper into the room. Glancing over at Derrick and Claudine, he continued. "What have we got so far?"

"The sniper was definitely a pro," Max answered first. "But he made a dumb move. He left the launch tube behind in the blind."

"Good," Jake told him. Track the serial number."

"Already on it," Max said grinning at him.

"Speaking of tracking. We did manage to track the guy to the road on the crest of the hill," Derrick said with a slight shrug of his shoulders. "But he must have had a car waiting for him there. Because there was no sign of him anywhere once we reached the road."

Jake turned to Claudine, "What are Moreau and his people saying?"

"Nothing. They're blaming the explosion on a gas leak."

"What about Bill?" Riley asked her. "What did they say about him."

Claudine shook her head at her as she said, "They're not identifying him. At least not publicly."

As Riley and Jake exchanged looks, she continued, "All they're reporting is that an unidentified body was discovered in the wreckage after the fire. And due to the fire damage they are unable to determine if the body is a male or female at this time."

"Well," Jake said. "That's one way to not release his identity."

"But why are they doing that?" Riley asked. "Whoever killed him knew who he was."

"It's a feint," Derrick explained to her. "They don't want the killer and his associates to realize what they know."

"But the question is," Jake said, "do they know anything."

"Or do they think Riley had something to do with it," Claudine said.

"Me!?!" Riley said to her. Catching the thoughtful look on everyone's faces she protested. "How can they think I was involved?"

She turned to Jake, "I was with you the whole time."

"But they don't know that," Apollo said as he and Max joined the group.

"If the body was toasted bad enough. They honestly may not know if they're dealing with a male or female corpse," Max added.

"Max is right," Derrick said to Riley. "It's possible that the police haven't been able to identify the body yet."

"So they think it could be me?"

"No," Claudine said giving Riley a quick shake of her head. "*Inspecteur* Moreau called while you were busy in the dispensary sewing up Jake."

Jake nodded in silent agreement.

Nodding, Claudine continued, "Since you were busy at the moment, I didn't think that you were particularly anxious to speak with him."

"I'm not," Jake said.

"That's why I let him believe you were showing Riley the sights." Claudine grinned at Jake. "And that you left your cell phone here so you couldn't be disturbed."

"Did he believe you?" Jake asked.

"About the cell phone? *Non.* About wanting to be alone with Riley, of course. After all, he is a Frenchman, you know."

Riley could feel herself blushing all the way down to her roots as Jake's companions enjoyed a laugh on him.

Claudine was surprisingly closer to the truth than he had realized until just now, Jake thought. Looking at the pink flush on Riley's cheeks he was startled to discover that he wanted to reach out and softly stoke those cheeks. And lean close enough to smell the sweet scent of her silken hair.

Blinking hard to clear his mind of that vision and to focus his attention back on the matter at hand, Jake said to Derrick, "What about our contact in the police lab? Do we have anything on the round that was fired?"

A gleam of satisfaction filled Derrick's eyes. "That we do."

Jake and the others watched as Derrick crossed back to the console to collect a report and return with it in hand. "It was an old Soviet anti-tank round," Derrick read. Looking up at Jake and Riley, he continued, " The kind they were using in Afghanistan."

"Any idea where it came from?"

Derrick shook his head. "Hard to say. The Taliban had stockpiles of the things all over the place after the Russians pulled out in 1989."

"You can pick them up on the international arms market for a dime," Max said from his workstation.

"Great," Jake said in disgust. "It looks like that's going to be a dead end."

"What about Bill's date?" Riley asked.

Her question caught Jake and the others off-guard.

"What about her?"

"The Bill Larson I worked with wasn't the kind of guy to be associating with people who fire anti-tank rockets at other people."

Riley shook her head at Jake as she continued. "Despite all of his bragging about being a Green Beret. The closet Bill ever came to seeing any action was handing out parachutes to the rest of his battalion."

"Okay," Jake said in encouragement.

"With his gambling problems I can see him going to the casino," she said. "But with all of his money problems I doubt if he could have even afforded to buy a cup of coffee there. Much less place any bets."

"Or picking up an expensive hooker," a grinning Jake finished for her.

Riley nodded at him. "Exactly."

"We know who she is," Claudine said. "Gabrielle LeFleuer," Claudine walked over to her console and picked up one of the sheets of paper. Glancing at it she returned to Jake's side with the page in her hand.

"And she's on the list for us to talk to," she said handing the page to Jake.

"We need to put her at the head of the list," Jake said as he glanced at Claudine's information.

"Do you think she'll know anything about who tried to kill us?" Riley asked.

"There's no telling until we talk to her," Jake said.

"Then let's go talk to her. I want to hear what she has to say."

Claudine shot Jake a quick glance.

Catching that glance, Riley gave the two of them a hard look. "Look, using arson to cover up a robbery I can understand. But using a rocket launcher to cover up a murder is more than a bit extreme," Riley said with an edge to her voice. "Even for a place as over the top as Monaco is."

Amused, Derrick bit down on the inside of his cheek as he watched Jake exchange heavy glances with Claudine.

"Stealing the diamond, I can understand. Using the fire to cover the theft and accidentally - or deliberately- killing the people in the penthouse," Riley continued. "I can understand. Maybe."

Throwing her hands palms up to emphasis her point, Riley said. "But why kill Bill Larson? And why use a rocket launcher against us when the shooter could have simply waited for us to exit the building." She shook her head in frustration, "That just seems to be extremely over-the-top for a simple robber. Don't you think?"

Riley locked eyes with Jake as she continued. "You might know people like that. But I can guarantee you that I most certainly don't."

Jake silently returned her stare.

"There's a good chance that I'm going to go to prison for a very long time for what they did."

Riley paused to look at everyone in the room, one by one, as she continued. "So, we can either work together as a team. Or…."

"'Or' what?" Jake said as she returned her gaze to him.

"Or," she said to him, "I'll go looking for them on my own."

Jake laughed and shook his head. "You're a nurse. What do you know about tracking down killers."

Riley was a motionless as a stone.

"More than you may ever realize," she said softly. "And I've got an ace up my sleeve that you don't."

The amusement vanished from Jake's eyes. "And that would be?"

"Me." Riley said as Jake's companions shifted uncomfortably. "Whoever they are, it's clear as day that they can't afford to have me talking."

"But you don't know anything," Claudine interrupted.

Turning to Claudine, Riley give her a brief smile. "But they don't know that."

Turning back toward Jake, she continued. "Do they?"

Returning Jake's steady gaze Riley said, "So. Do we work together as a team, or not?"

CHAPTER 16

The silence in the room was deafening as Jake returned Riley's determined glare.

He blinked first.

"Give her the bloody information," he told Claudine from behind clenched teeth.

Shaking his head at a grinning Riley as she reached for the paper Claudine was handing to her, he continued. "Pig-headed, that's what you are."

Riley shook her head back at him. "No. Determined."

"They make a cute couple," Max whispered into Apollo's ear.

"I heard that," Jake rumbled back at him as he watched Riley read quickly through the data sheet on Gabrielle LeFleuer.

Finishing the page, Riley looked back up at Jake. "She really is very expensive, isn't she."

Jake nodded in response as Riley, lightly tapping the page in her hand with her forefinger, looked away lost in thought.

Jake kept the scowl on his face in order to hide his thoughts. With her spunk, no wonder she survived that fire, he thought as he watched the thoughts skimming across her face. I wonder if she knows how beautiful she is.

Jake quickly looked around to see if he had accidentally spoken out loud.

Derrick and Claudine had moved off to look at one of the nearby monitors. And Max and Apollo were working at their separate workstations. Only Riley was close enough to have heard him. And judging by the thoughtful frown scrunching her eyebrows together she wasn't paying the least bit of attention to him. Thank the stars for that. The last thing he need right now was to make an utter fool of himself.

Riley suddenly shifted her attention back to him.

"Bill never mentioned it at all to me," she said. "But I'm wondering if he'd ever been to the casino before that night."

"He hadn't," Jake answered her. "We checked with the security people there. That was the one and only time he'd ever been there."

"Then he's going there is really odd," she said slightly shaking her head at him. "Because the folks there were clearly out of his league from every angle."

"Agreed."

"Can we look at that security video again?"

"Yes," Jake said. "Are you looking for anything in particular?"

Riley shook her head at him. "I don't know what I'm looking for."

As Jake led her over to a nearby monitor and keyed up the video, she continued. "I'm just hoping that something will pop out for me."

Standing next to Jake as he entered keyboard commands to bring up the video, Riley was uncomfortably aware of him at her side. Keeping her eyes focused on the keyboard and monitor she couldn't help notice how broad and strong his hands where. That he kept his nails clipped short. And that the sun had bleached the fine hairs on the backs of his deeply tanned hands.

The man wasn't paying the least bit of attention to her, but Riley felt her heart thumping in her chest. And she noticed how she had to repeatedly catch her breath because it was suddenly so shallow. What in the world was the matter with her? The only reason he even noticed that she was alive was because she was irritating the living daylights out of him by getting in his face.

But what did he expect? What did the others expect? It was her freedom that was on the line – not theirs.

"OK," Jake intruded into the whirlpool of her thoughts. "Here we go." With a simple mouse click he brought up the security video of Bill Larson entering the lobby of the Monte Carlo Casino.

Staring intently at the figures on the monitor Riley tried to focus all of her attention on them. But for some reason, totally beyond her comprehension, she flashed back to the feeling of his strong lips against hers. And the way the warmth of his kiss flooded through her entire body like the leading edge of an incoming tide.

"Well," Jake's voice pulled her back to the present. "Did you see anything?"

"Wha…"

"Did anything jumped out at you in the video?"

"Uhm, no. Uh, can we run through it again?"

Giving her a half shrug with his right shoulder, Jake started the sequence rolling again.

Only this time all of Riley's attention was riveted onto the screen and the two figures filling center stage.

Once again Riley couldn't help feeling sorry for Bill Larson in his worn corduroy sports jacket and cheap slacks. He looked so out of place among the tuxedoed and heavily jeweled glitterati crowd swirling around him. The few who deigned to notice him at all gave him wide berth as they flowed around him as they moved across the crowded lobby.

"He doesn't look that bad," Riley commented in his defense as she watched Larson standing in the middle of the crowded lobby scanning the crowd as if for a familiar face.

"What can you tell me about Gabrielle LeFleuer," Riley said as the woman in question turned from chatting with a rotund, white-haired older man to scan the area near the lobby doors without spotting Larson.

"She likes to be seen in all of the right places with all of the right people," Jake said in an ironic tone that caused Riley to throw him a quick glance before turning her eyes back to the monitor screen.

"What does she do for a living?"

"You mean aside from being a full time 'escort'?"

"Call girl, you mean." Riley said as she watched Bill reached Gabrielle's side and she leaned forward to give him an eyeful of her cleavage as she said something to him.

"She's never been busted for that as far as we've been able to find out."

"Then how does she get paid?" Riley asked as the video Gabrielle slipped her left arm through the crook Bill's right one and they started for the Casino's front doors.

"According to Gabrielle, she only dates 'friends,'" Jake explained.

"Oh, you mean "friends" who take "care" of her," Riley said as she shot him another quick glance. "That must be nice for her."

Turning back to the video, Riley saw Gabrielle flutter her garishly long eyelashes at the clearly bedazzled Larson as they approached the exit.

"It is," Jake said. "Especially when her friends turn out to be multi-millionaires and billionaires – Middle Eastern oil sheiks, Russian oil barons, and an occasional Formula One winner now and then to liven things up."

"How did she know?" Riley said as she suddenly straightened up to turn and face him.

"How rich they are?"

"No," Riley said shaking her head and pointing to the still playing security video of Larson and Gabrielle exiting the casino together. "How did she know to target Larson?"

Jake gives her a blank look.

"I'm mean look at her," Riley said freezing the video. "She's gorgeous and as deadly as a cobra. Yet she made a beeline for him the moment she spotted him standing there looking like a geek caught in some bully's headlights."

Jake could only shrug at her in response.

"I mean, come on," Riley said shaking her head in disbelief. "I worked with the man for six months. And believe me when I tell you that there was not one thing about him that would attract a woman of Gabrielle's caliber."

"The only thing that attracts her is power and money," Jake said.

"And Bill definitely didn't have either one."

Jake glanced at the freeze frame of Gabrielle LeFleuer and Bill Larson approaching the casino's lobby exit doors. Clicking off the video feed he turned back to Riley. "That's why we checking out Gabrielle now."

"Larson clearly couldn't cover her tab," Jake continued. "So we're digging into her business to see which of her "friends" might have a reason to set that meet up."

"You don't think he actually spent the night with her like he claimed?"

Jake pursed his lower lip. "Anything is possible. This is Monaco."

Riley looked around the room at the others who were all busily engaged at their various computers and monitor screens.

"We need to go talk to Gabrielle."

"We're planning on it."

"We need to talk to her now," Riley said turning her full attention on him. "She could be in danger from whoever tried to kill us."

It was Jake's turn to look around at his companions before turning back to her. "We will talk to her as soon as we have a little more information to work with."

"It might be too late then," Riley insisted.

Jake reached out to put a steadying hand on her shoulder. "You saw what happened with Larson and us," he said soothingly. "We need information so we can know what to expect when we do go to talk to her. Otherwise, we could be walking into another ambush."

Dipping his head slightly to be able to look her directly in the eye, he continued. "And that one we might not be lucky enough to walk away from in one piece."

With him close enough to kiss, Riley had to fight her natural urge to reach out and run her finger gently over his lower lip.

"It's foolish for us to go charging into a situation blind," Riley heard him say from a distance that had nothing to do with the physical space between them. "The more info we have, the better prepared we are to question her and know if she's lying to us."

Jake straightened back up his full height. "Agreed?" he said.

"What?" Riley said finally tearing her eyes away from his lips. For a brief, terrifying second, she had the feeling that he knew exactly what she had been thinking.

But a flashing glance up at his face thankfully immediately dispelled that horrifying thought.

What in the world is the matter with you! Riley thought as she gave Jake an abbreviated nod in response to his comments. If the local cop has his way, she could be sitting in a French jail cell for most of her natural life. And for something she didn't do.

And she didn't care how sexually attractive Jake Rafferty was. She darn well better remember that it's not her freedom and happiness he's concerned with in the least. Yep, she better not forget that the only thing she represented to Jake Rafferty and his friends was bait on the hoof.

Mentally bending over and pulling up her socks and straightening her spine, Riley returned Jake's gaze before giving him a curt nod of acknowledgment.

"Okay, I understand," she said as she did a quick visual survey of the room around her. As her eyes swept over the room behind Jake, she spotted what she had been hoping to find. And luckily for her, it was conveniently located near the door.

Refocusing all of her attention on Jake, she gave him a reassuring smile that was as real as his play acting concern for her was. "I may not be happy about waiting," she said with complete honesty.

"But I'll go along with whatever you say," she continued with all of her fingers and toes mentally crossed.

Liar, liar, her conscience shouted in her inner ear, but she ignored it completely as she continued to smile reassuringly at an unsuspecting Jake.

"How's your shoulder doing?" she asked deftly changing the subject.

Gingerly grabbing his immobilized elbow the pain in Jake's eyes belied his words. "It's doing fine."

"Why don't you at least let me give you another shot for the pain. It'll help take some of that edge off."

Jake shook his head at her. "Thanks, but I've got work I need to do here. And that would only slow me down."

"You're sure?" Riley said with genuine concern. He might be using her for bait, but she was still a nurse and genetically could not ignore another human in pain. Not if there was anything she could do to ease it.

Suddenly realizing that he was unconsciously rubbing his aching forearm, Jake suddenly dropped his right hand to let it hang by his side. "What about you?" he said to her. "I didn't see you taking anything to help with the pain you must be in too."

Riley was genuinely surprised to realize that Jake was right. She had been so busy tending to him and Apollo that she had completely forgotten all about the various cuts, bruises and abrasions she had suffered in the rocket explosion.

"Oh, I'm all right. I'm tougher than I look. I took a couple of aspirins and I'll be just fine," she said.

Throwing a quick glance at the door behind him, Riley then turned back to Jake. "If you're going to be tied up here awhile, I'll think I'll take advantage of that and go soak in a hot tub."

"Of course," Jake said. "I can have Claudine lend you a hand if you need some help."

Riley let out a laugh and shook her head at him. "Thanks, but I can manage."

She turned to go, but then stopped and turned back to Jake. "You'll call me if there's anything I can do to help."

"Yes," Jake said. "Of course."

"Thanks. I'll talk to you in a little while."

Turning, Riley started for the door. Jake watched her for a moment or two and then turned to join Derrick and Claudine up on the platform area.

Approaching the door, Riley gave a slight turn of her head. From the corner of her eye she confirmed that Jake's attention was no longer on her. Moving casually she reached out as she was approaching the door and snagged one of the sets of car keys hanging on a hook near the door.

Holding her breath she continued towards the door – waiting for someone to raise the alarm. But only the busy hum from the banks of electronic equipment and the soft murmurs of voices could be heard behind her.

Rolling her eyes skyward in relief, she hurried out of the door with only one purpose in mind.

And it definitely wasn't soaking in a hot tub of bubbles.

CHAPTER 17

Gabrielle LeFleuer's apartment was located on the tenth floor of a modern, twelve-storey pink sandstone high rise in sight of Monaco's royal palace. Sprawled at its feet was the luxury yacht-filled new harbor. Pulling up across from its entrance Riley saw no sign of a bellman or security guard in the ornate lobby.

She had to circle the block three times before she finally was able to slip into an empty curbside parking place two doors down from Gabrielle's building. Using the electronic fob to lock the doors of Jake's borrowed SUV, Riley approached the glass fronted lobby with caution. But luck was on her side because there was still no sign of a bellman or lobby security guard.

Hurrying up the canopied walkway, she spotted the ceiling mounted security camera tucked into the corner of the lobby. Keeping her face turned away from the camera she entered the lobby and boldly headed for the bank of two shiny elevators. Reaching them she confidently punched the up button. All the while making sure to keep her face turned away from the camera lens.

The moment the elevator door opened she was inside and pushing the button marked with a big "10". It wasn't until the elevator doors slid close that she finally let out a big breath of relief. The ride up to the tenth floor was a straight shot and she stepped out into the sunlit lobby in under a minute.

Thank heavens for Claudine's data sheet she thought as she checked the hallway marker for apartment 1011. Now all she had to do was hope like crazy that Gabrielle spoke English because her French was two words up from non-existing. A fact Étienne Devereux had teased her about unmercifully.

Gabrielle's apartment was halfway down the main corridor and facing the sunny harbor. With the thick woolen carpet muffling her footsteps Riley approached the apartment as silently as a ghost. As she reached the door to 1011, she was surprised to see that it was open about a foot.

Maybe she's in the laundry room Riley thought as she approached the open apartment door. Looking over her shoulder in both directions Riley didn't see anything to indicate that there was a laundry room on this floor. Or if there was even one in the building.

Shrugging it off she reached out and lightly knocked on the partially open door. "Hello, Gabrielle."

Silence was all that answered her call. So she knocked harder and called out in a louder voice. "Miss LeFleuer, are you home?"

There was no response, but the force of her knock swung the door wide enough for Riley to spot the form of a dark-haired woman sprawled on the living room floor at the end of the long entry hallway leading from the open door.

"Gabrielle?" Riley called out as she started to go to the fallen woman's aid. There were two open doorways lining the right side of the entry hallway as Riley stepped through the open door. A waist-high, arched fronted, antique cabinet filled the space between the two open side doors. On its top was a tall clear crystal vase of sunny yellow daffodils and white ruffled irises. A verdigris copper figurine of a pirouetting dancer and a heavy paperweight of clear glass filled with a blue iris rested at the base of the flower vase.

148

Focused on the woman Riley barely noted her surroundings as she hurried past the first open doorway on her way towards the sun filled living room. The first hint of danger came from the slight sense of movement she caught out of the corner of her eye. But before she could even turn her head, a thin metal loop dropped over her head.

Instinctively, Riley threw up her left forearm to protect her face. She managed to slide her arm between the side of her face and the metal loop just as the metal loop was jerked tight. The razor thin wire cut deep into the middle of her arm.

Garrote her mind screamed as she immediately fell back against her unseen assailant in order to lessen his angle of attack.

Fear surged through her with the speed of a passing freight train and it momentarily blacked out her vision. Her forearm was pinned like a vise against the side of her face as her assailant relentlessly pulled the wire loop tighter and tighter around her neck.

Heaving backwards, the assailant hauled her so far back that only the tips of her toes had contact with the floor. All the while he kept pulling the loop tighter and tighter.

Riley couldn't breathe and her mouth was filling with blood from the gash she bit into the side of her tongue. A thin circle of blinding yellow light was ringing the black disc blocking her eyes. With her back arced like a bent willow bow she had no contact with the floor for any leverage. She clawed desperately to get her free right hand under the wire painfully cutting into her raw throat but it was buried too deep in her swollen flesh for her to be able to work her fingers under it.

Flailing out with her right arm Riley struck the crystal vase of flowers. Above the Niagara Falls of a roar filling her ears she heard the faint tinkle of glass shattering. But what caught her attention was the back of her hand brushing a sharp metal object.

Grasping it in her fist, with all of her rapidly waning strength she swung her right arm over the side of her head and made contact with the assailant.

The roaring in her ears was deafening so she couldn't be sure if she had heard him grunt in pain or not. But she was sure that there was a momentary release of pressure on her throat and trapped forearm. So she struck again, and again, and again. With the fourth blow her attacker lost his hold on the wire embedded in her throat.

That was all the advantage available and she took it.

Staggered by her blows, the assailant had allowed her to slip low enough for her feet to make contact with the floor beneath her. Still unable to see around the black discs blocking her vision, Riley used her sense of smell to locate the man by the coppery scent of the blood pouring from his wounds where she had stabbed him with the metal figurine still tightly clutched in her right hand.

Feeling the body heat emanating from him she centered on his mass and brought the weapon down with all the force she had left. This time she definitely heard his grunt of pain and he fell back into the room behind him.

She still couldn't see anything but the two black discs floating in front of her eyes. But the faint breeze blowing in from the open front door gave her the sense of direction she so desperately needed.

Stumbling from pain and panic Riley staggered out into the corridor.

"Help me!" she tried to scream but no sound could make its way out of her swollen throat.

Using the wall as her guide she staggered towards the bank of elevators she knew were located in the middle of the corridor. By the time she reached them she was finally able to see. But she still was deaf due to the roaring in her ears.

Frantically pounding both elevator buttons she sobbed frantically, "Hurry! Hurry! Oh, please hurry!"

A sudden crash from inside of Gabrielle's apartment turned her blood as cold as arctic ice. Desperately whipping her head back and forth in search of anything she could use as a weapon, the only thing she could see was the scarlet hue of the fire alarm bell mounted near the elevator bank.

Staggering over to it she yanked it down and instantly the ear piercing shrieks of the fire alarm bell echoed throughout the entire floor. But still there was no sign of an elevator car.

Gulping air down her raw throat, Riley fought to control her panic. Blinking back the tears that were suddenly spilling down her face she once again searched the corridor for anything she could use as a weapon to save her life.

She couldn't find anything. She wanted desperately to wait for the elevator but if the assailant came after her a second time she knew all the way down into her bones that he would succeed in killing her.

If she was going to live she had to move.

It was as simple as that.

Turning away from Gabrielle's open apartment door Riley stumbled down the opposite corridor on rubbery legs that threatened to collapse under her at any second.

Thirty feet from the elevator banks she stumbled across a five foot deep alcove that contained a metal door. Throwing herself against it she pushed it open to discover a metal set of fire escape stairs.

She was just about to start down them when she realized that in her present condition the killer could easily outrun her. *Think!* Her mind screamed out at her. *Use your brains to outwit his brawn* her father's childhood lesson echoed down through the years and brought her up short.

Sobbing in fear she swung back towards the waiting corridor. Edging to the alcove opening she cautiously peered one eye around the edge to check out the corridor leading from Gabrielle's apartment.

It was still empty.

Clamping her right hand over her mouth to muffle her sobs, she stumbled towards her end of the corridor searching for another escape route. Rounding the corner her eyes widened in disbelief. It was a dead end!

A muffled sound from Gabrielle's doorway sent her staggering down towards the plain wooden door she could see along the left side of the corridor. Reaching it she turned the knob but it was locked.

Her chest heaving with suppressed sobs Riley swung around and was about to collapse in despair when she realized that there was a large, covered metal chute located at waist level directly across from her. Staggering the three steps it took her to cross over to it, Riley pushed up the slide covering and found herself peering down into the darkness of an old dumb waiter shaft that had been converted into a garbage chute.

She was ready to cry from relief, but the sound of the fire stairwell door being flung open rocketed her onto the ledge of the dark, metal lined chute. Reaching out she discovered that it was less than three feet wide.

Turning herself around she braced her feet on either side of the opening and her back against the opposite wall. Momentarily leaning slightly forward she was able to slide the cover back down into place.

Her first instinct was to start inching down the chute.

No, she told herself. If he gets this far, that's the first place he'd expect me to be.

Pulling in a deep lungful of air, and with her feet still bracketing the now closed opening, Riley cradled her injured left arm against her chest and began to slowly inch her way upward. As soon as her feet cleared the opening, she began to move on a diagonal until she was pressing against the far corner of the chute where the shadows were the darkest.

Fearing that the light spilling in when the cover was lifted might reveal her, Riley painfully kept inching her way upwards. It seemed like she had barely made any progress at all when she heard the muffled crash of the assailant trying to open the locked door across from the chute. Through the walls she could hear his indistinct curses. But she couldn't tell what language he was speaking. Only that it was not French.

Pressing herself tight against the corner wall Riley closed her eyes tight, pressed her face to the wall, and tried to slow her breathing. She knew from nursing school and personal experience that animals and humans instinctively know when someone is looking at them. She began sending up silent prayers that the assailant didn't have a flashlight with him. If he did, it would be all over for her.

Just as that thought entered her mind, the chute cover was wrenched upward and she heard the assailant shove his upper torso into the opening. Fighting the urge to peek down at him, Riley held her breath and willed her muscles to stone. But her racing heart ignored her completely and its echo in her ears sounded as loud as a kettle drum during a football half time show.

Snarling like a wounded beast, the assailant stared down into the inky depths of the chute as he listened for any sound of movement under the piercing shriek of the still ringing fire alarm bell ricocheting along the length of the corridor behind him. When he found only silence from the depths before him, he quickly glanced upwards to find nothing but more blackness as deep as a Siberian coal mine. Howling like a demented beast, he withdrew from the opening and slammed the covering back into place.

CHAPTER 18

As the silence of the shaft enveloped her, an icy chill suddenly flooded Riley's entire body as the adrenaline that had been surging through her dissipated like a river rushing through a broken dam. Wrapping both arms as tight around herself as she could Riley tried to stop the heat leaching out of her body as she trembled with uncontrollable shakes.

Unable to control her trembling muscles, and too weak to move, Riley drew in gulps of air like a woman drowning. I'm going to die here and nobody will ever know she thought in despair as she closed her eyes and her head fell back against the wall behind her.

Suddenly was a muffled rumble and the metal walls lining the chute momentarily fluttered against her back.

What was that? Riley's eyes darted open in alarm. Another rocket?

But the blackness around her was undisturbed. And the chute walls were motionless.

Slowly, like the tide smoothing a rock, her jagged breathing started to even out and the tremblings eased. But she was still too weak to move.

Good move Copper, she thought. This is a heck of a mess you've gotten yourself into this time. And what are you going to do to get yourself out of it?

Slowly twisting her head forward Riley peered into the darkness beneath her hoping for a hint of light from the shaft's opening. All she found was soul stealing blackness. Softly thunking her head back against the wall behind her Riley closed her eyes against the void over her head. Think Riley, she chided herself. Use your brain. That's what it's there for. She could still hear her Dad telling her that more times than she could count when she was growing up. What do you have to do to get yourself out of this jam?

ADD it up - she thought as a spark flickered faintly somewhere deep in the recesses of her memories. You know how do to that. You'd better - given the number of times that you have had to do it over the years.

Assess.

Decide.

Do it.

Opening her eyes to the darkness around her, Riley steadied her breathing and found her resolve.

She had never been afraid of the dark. In fact, she found it comforting, maybe because she had been born with uncanny night vision. Even in the darkest night her eyes were able to pick up the merest hint of light if it was present. Like here in this chute.

Looking around her all she saw at first was inky blackness. But as she looked below her where the opening should be, it was different. It was still black as pitch just like the rest of the shaft. But if she let her eyes relax, a ripple disturbance in the blackness slowly coalesced into a razor thin hint of lightness. And if she looked long enough, the almost invisible lightness slowly brightened to the faintest impression of actual light.

Raising her head to peer upward toward the top of the chute, Riley's brain whirled. The assailant would be expecting her to escape from the building. But, more than likely, he was expecting her to use the building's ground floor exits.

It was a twelve storey building and she was near the ceiling of the tenth floor. With only two floors and the roof above her, it didn't take a genius to figure out that it was a lot shorter distance to travel up to find an exit than the ten storeys beneath her.

Now all she had to do was to decide. Up or down?

Yeah, like that was really a hard decision to make.

So up it was, and move she did.

~~~

Slowly at first. Inch by inch she ascended. As the warmth returned to her body and muscles, the smoother her movements became. At the same time her confidence was also returning. And with it her anger.

Not anger, she thought. Fury.

She had to admit it whether she liked it or not. She had been flat out terrified. Maybe even the most terrified she had ever been in her life.

Never had she felt so utterly helpless in her entire life.

She absolutely hated that feeling with every fiber of her being. That and the man who had done that to her. The attack had been brutal. But the terror and the feeling of utter helplessness she experienced was far worse. And she didn't know if she would ever recover from it.

That was what she hated the most.

The hidden damage of terror.

~~~

When she had reached the floor above, Riley had already decided to by-pass floors eleven and twelve and head for the roof instead. While her assailant knew what she looked like, she had never gotten so much of a glimpse of his features. And since he had been wearing black leather gloves – the only thing she had noticed about him during the attack - that and the fact that he was as strong as a 12' tall grizzly. But now, she realized, that meant that she couldn't even identify him by his hands.

She definitely didn't want to take a chance of running into him if he was searching those floors for her. So the roof was her best option. There she'd be able to see if anyone was lurking to attack her. And she could use it to access the neighboring buildings that she would use to reach the street and make her escape.

~~~

Walking out of the front door of the building four buildings away from Gabrielle's, Riley was physically exhausted but more determined than ever to unravel the mystery behind Étienne Devereux's murder. And she was as equally convinced that there was far more than just a simple robbery behind the events. Yes, $157 million was a lot of money, she thought. But surely there would be more than enough to go around once the stolen necklace had been fenced.

So why murder Gabrielle LeFleuer?

She certainly could understand them killing Bill Larson since he wasn't sophisticated enough to keep quiet about what he knew. But from the little she knew about Gabrielle, Riley knew that the woman was smart and used to dealing with men with a lot of money and power. While it was not a way of life Riley would be comfortable living, she had to admit that Gabrielle LeFleuer just seemed too smart to jeopardize the lifestyle she had worked so hard to build.

So, again she had to ask herself, why murder Gabrielle?

Just for a necklace?

And what about Étienne Devereux's death?

The man was a billionaire for heaven's sake. He was worth far more in ransom than his wife's necklace. So why didn't the robbers snatch him instead? Or, at least in addition to the necklace. Why leave him to die like they had done?

Again, it just didn't make sense.

Carmela and I were merely 'collateral damage' as the military would call it, she thought. But Étienne Devereux as simple collateral damage for someone sophisticated enough to pull off the robbery that just did not make any sense at all.

If money was the object of the robbery Étienne's billions beat out Constanza's mere millions any day of the week.

So the real question she needed to answer if she was going to clear her name was – what in the world were the robbers really after?

CAROL A. HUGHES

CHAPTER 19

Pulling her blouse up around her neck as far as she could to hide the blood encrusted ring of raw and bruised flesh encircling her neck, Riley avoided eye contact with the few people she passed on her short trip to her parked SUV. Using the key fob, she released the locks as she hurried towards the vehicle.

Just as she reached the driver's door a Black SUV screeched to a halt next to her. From behind the wheel Apollo's still battered face grinned at her through the open passenger's side window.

"You might want to get in before Inspector Moreau or one of his people spots you."

When she hesitated, he shrugged a shoulder at her. "It's either this or hope that you don't run into Jake. Because he's mad enough right now to wring your neck for taking off like you did."

Throwing a wary glance around at the passing traffic and pedestrians in search of a sign of her attacker, Riley's unconsciously raised her right hand to protect her battered throat. With a last quick look she nodded at Apollo and scrambled into the passenger seat next to him.

"I'd really hate to see what shape the other guy is in," Apollo said shaking his head at her as he checked his rear view mirror before pulling out into the traffic flowing past them.

Riley gave him a tight smile in return.

"Are you OK?" he asked.

"Ask me when this is all over."

"Deal," he said giving her a quick wink before turning his head to check his side mirror.

"So what is it with you and burning buildings?" he continued as his eyes searched for a break in the traffic.

"What?"

Spotting a slight break in the oncoming traffic he whipped a swift U-turn and headed back towards Gabrielle's high rise. Throwing Riley a quick glance and seeing her peering intently at him, he pointed through the windshield towards the rapidly approaching high rise with its fire marred wall of what she knew was Gabrielle's apartment.

"What happened?" she asked as Apollo slowed to edge past the gaggle of police and fire vehicles clustered in front of the building. Several uniformed police officers were directing traffic past the parked fire and rescue vehicles where the fire crews were busily reloading their equipment.

Pulling up to a policemen directing traffic past the driveway leading to the building's underground garage, Apollo paused to speak to him.

"Inspector Moreau is expecting us," he said. As he did, Riley nervously scanned the crowd of curious on-lookers being held at bay behind the crime scene tape blocking the sidewalk in front of the building.

Thankfully no one was paying the slightest attention to her.

Giving Apollo a silent nod the policeman pointed for him to park on the residents' driveway.

Apollo did so and they both climbed out of the vehicle and headed for the door to the building's lobby. As they hurried towards it, Apollo used his bulk to shield her from the curiosity of the on-lookers and the blinding flashes of the paparazzi's cameras. At the same time she was continually scanning the crowd.

"Do you see him?"

"Who?" she said as they approached the lobby door guarded by a uniformed policeman.

"Your wrestling mate," he said as they reached the officer.

Before she could answer, Apollo nodded at the police officer and once again explained, "Inspector Moreau is expecting us."

Giving them a clipped nod, the officer turned his eyes back to the street in front of him as Apollo opened the door for her and they stepped into the now crowded lobby.

Bright spotlights on telescoping tripod poles drenched the small lobby in blinding light. Crime scene technicians, uniformed police officers, two coroner's assistants and a deputy coroner filled the lobby to capacity. As Apollo spoke with the cop logging in all visitors, Riley spotted a technician on a stepladder removing the lobby's security camera. As he started down the short ladder, she realized that the lens had been shot out.

"OK," Apollo said turning to her. "We're clear to go upstairs."

As he guided her across the crowded lobby, Riley noticed something else she had not noticed when she was there earlier. The bright halogen work lights revealed the spray of blood splatter that had dried on the white marble wall behind the security desk.

Seeing her registering the blood that had dribbled down the wall Apollo told her quietly as they approached the waiting elevator, "The security guard is behind the desk."

Nodding as she turned towards the elevator, Riley said, "Is there anybody else besides Gabrielle?"

"I don't know yet."

A uniformed police woman was playing elevator operator so they rode to the tenth floor in silence. As they did, both Riley and Apollo used the mirror-like surface of the metal walls to check out their various injuries.

Winking at the curious police woman who was eyeing their various injuries, Apollo said to the back of her head, "We've been in the gym working out."

Riley had to bite back an unexpected smile as the embarrassed officer nodded the back of her head at them.

When they reached the tenth floor and the elevator door opened, Riley would have remained rooted in her spot if Apollo hadn't placed his hand on the small of her back and given her the gentlest of nudges to get her moving.

"This might get dicey," Apollo whispered at her as they approached Gabrielle's apartment with its still open door. Only this time there was a uniformed police officer with a clipboard logging everyone entering the room.

"So you just might want to follow my lead," he cautioned as they walked up to the waiting policeman who had been warily watching their approach.

"Inspector Moreau is expecting us," Apollo repeated for a third time.

While Apollo was taking care of signing them in on the visitor's roster, Riley peered down the long hallway for a second time in just hours. The sunlight was still filling the living room at end of the hallway like before. Only now the walls of both the hallway and the living room were charred and streaked with soot and water stains. From what she could see of the living room, it was in shambles from a massive explosion that appeared to have originated in the room off the second open doorway in the hallway. And now the body on the floor was covered with a canvas tarp. That is all except for the manicured hand poking out from under the edge of the tarp.

She spotted Moreau talking to Jake as they stood several feet back from the body. Glancing up, Jake spotted her but never let on to Moreau, who had his back to the door as he stood talking to Jake. Despite his appearance of non-response, even across the distance Riley could sense the mixture of contained anger, relief and surprise that momentarily flashed across his eyes when he spotted her with Apollo.

Finished with the officer Apollo turned back to her. "Can you do this?"

She shot him a flinty look. "I was a combat nurse. I've seen a dead body or two in my time."

Apollo grinned down at her. "I knew you were tough."

Riley turned and started down the hallway towards the body with Apollo on her heels.

As they stepped into the room, Moreau turned at the sound of their arrival. Riley saw the flash of alarm in Jake's eyes as both men took note of her various injuries. But both quickly masked their reactions.

"Hey, boss," Apollo said from over her shoulder. "Sorry it took us so long. But we were at the gym when your call came in."

"Gym?" Moreau said never taking his eyes off of Riley who returned his stare. Over his shoulder she had a clear view of Jake watching her just as intensely.

Before she could respond, Apollo casually laid his hand on her right shoulder in warning.

"We were practicing our martial arts moves," he said to Moreau as he and Riley edged around the body to join Jake at Moreau's side. "I guess we both got a little carried away with ourselves."

"Is that Gabrielle LeFleuer?" Riley asked Moreau.

"*Oui*," Moreau said as he stared at her injured throat along with Jake.

Lightly touching her raw neck Riley gave Moreau an open look as she laughed slightly. "It looks worse than it is, Inspector."

Moreau looked over at Apollo's battered face. "She did that to you?"

Apollo looked genuinely sheepish. "I'm never going to live it down."

Moreau turned back to Riley with a look of genuine respect on his face. "You certainly are an interesting woman, Miss Copper."

Riley shrugged at him. "Well, when you're the only girl growing up on a cattle ranch, you've got to know how to deal with all those drunken cowboys on paydays."

Moreau nodded back at her. As he did, she caught the subtle tension in Jake's face. She couldn't tell if he was concerned about her, or wanted to throttle her. At the moment she really didn't care which it was. All she really wanted to do was deal with her injuries and then fall into bed and sleep the next week away.

She didn't know if Apollo could read her mind or not. But she could have kissed him when he came to her rescue by asking Jake, "Boss was there a reason you wanted us here?"

"Actually, I'm the one who requested your presence," Moreau said before Jake could reply. He looked at Riley as he continued. "It was you that I wanted to talk to."

"Me?" Riley said genuinely surprised. "Why?"

When Moreau gave her a piercing look in response, Riley looked to Jake for guidance. But all he could do was shrug at her in reply.

Turning back to the silent Moreau, Riley felt her temper flare before she could stop it. "Wait a minute. Are you saying that you think I had something to do with this?"

"An arson fire, a dead body," Moreau said with a shrug.

"You can't be serious," Riley glared at him. "I've never even met the woman. So why in the world would you even think that I'd kill her?"

"Maybe because she provided your colleague with a solid alibi on the night of the Devereux fire."

Riley shook her head at Moreau, "You're too much Inspector, you really are. I didn't kill the woman. I hadn't even met her. And I don't know how this fire started. But I do know that no matter how it started, you won't be able to blame me for it because this time my fingerprints won't be on whatever was used to start the fire."

Jake surprised Riley by stepping to her side and interrupting Moreau. "Marcel, I can personally guarantee you that she isn't involved in this."

Riley couldn't tell who was more surprised – her or Moreau.

Jake grabbed her upper left arm, and instantly realized by the way she flinched that he had made a mistake. But he never broke eye contact with Moreau as he continued. "Now if you don't have any other questions, the three of us need to get back to the office. And Apollo and Riley here both need to take care of their injuries before they stiffen up and won't be able to move for the next couple of days."

Jake smiled pleasantly at Moreau. "Don't you agree?"

Moreau scrutinized his face with hawk-like eyes before reluctantly replying. "Your personal guarantee, you say?"

Jake nodded at his friend. "She's not involved. Meanwhile, I'll do some digging on my end and see if I can come up with anything that you might be able to use."

Apollo had moved to stand at Jake's side behind Riley. This time his hand on her shoulder was to keep her from swaying on her feet. She realized what he was doing and was so grateful that she was afraid that she'd burst into tears in front of Moreau despite her anger at him. So she bit the inside of her lower lip and put on her "poker face" while Moreau tried to decide what he was going to do about her.

"Marcel," Jake said. "You know where she is if you come up with any additional questions for her."

Moreau gave him the merest of nods in response while still watching Riley with his hawk eyes.

"If I were you, I'd try to figure out what else Gabrielle LeFleuer had in common with Bill Larson that got the both of them killed," Jake said.

Faster than a bullet train, Moreau shifted his full attention to Jake. "What do you know about Larson's murder?"

"Nothing," Jake said deftly covering his slip. "The news reported that a body was found in the rubble of that fire up at Devereux's garage."

Moreau's eyes were like two black marbles as he peered at Jake. "How did you know it was Devereux's garage. That wasn't in the news."

"I was the head of his security," Jake said. "I know about all of his properties. It was my job."

Moreau considered that for a moment before he gave a Jake the barest nod of acknowledgement. "How did you find out it was Larson's body we found?"

"Logic," Jake answered him. "I knew that he was staying with the chauffeur Maurice, who was at Cap-Ferrat with Constanza on the day of the fire. So that would have left Larson back at the apartment."

Moreau gave him a solid nod this time. "You are wasting your time in security. You'd make a fine cop."

Jake laughed and shook his head at him. "No thanks. Security pays way better than civil service."

He started to guide Riley out of the room with Apollo next to him. Reaching the hallway he ignored the body at their feet as he paused to say to Moreau, "Do you have any idea how much a quart of synthetic oil costs me for that Ferrari?"

Moreau laughed and shook his head at him.

Jake turned serious and indicated the body under the tarp. "Let me know if I can do anything to help you with this. She didn't deserve to die like that."

This time Moreau's nod was solemn.

Turning away from Moreau, Jake followed Riley and Apollo out to the elevator.

As they were waiting for it to arrive, Riley quietly asked, "How did she die?"

Jake kept his eyes locked on the indicator lights over the elevators. "She was garroted."

From the corner of his eye Apollo saw a shaken Riley subconsciously touch the wire marks around her own throat.

~~~

With the police woman still acting as the elevator operator, the ride to the ground floor was as silent as an empty well. Riley was lost in her own thoughts, but Apollo knew Jake well enough to feel the anger he was keeping a very tight lid on.

Catching Jake's eye in the reflection of the polished elevator walls, Apollo signaled for him to take a good look at Riley. She was fighting to stay on her feet and the dark circles of pain around her eyes were blacker than his own bruises. When Jake responded with a slight dip of his head, Apollo let out a breath he didn't realize that he had been holding in.

Jake led the way out of the building and straight over to Apollo's SUV. Riley let him walk her around to the passenger side without protesting that she didn't need any help. She didn't protest because the truth of the matter was, she knew that physically, she had hit the limit of her endurance.

As Apollo climbed behind the wheel, Jake opened the passenger door for her but she suddenly realized that she didn't have the strength to climb up into the cab.

Shaking her head she took a step back from the vehicle. "Can I ride with you instead?" she said to Jake.

Caught off-guard Jake and Apollo exchanged quick glances that Riley saw. "You're car is easier to fall into," she explained.

"So much for a Ferrari's sex appeal," Apollo laughed at Jake as he closed the passenger side door.

"Let everyone know that we're moving to *Le Brise,*" Jake said as he and Riley started towards his car that was parked at the curb in front of the next building.

"Any particular reason why?" Apollo asked.

"Moreau."

"Got it," Apollo said as he started out of the driveway. "We'll be set up in an hour."

But he was talking to Jake's back as he led Riley over to the nearby Ferrari.

CHAPTER 20

The Ferrari rocketed away from the curb and slipped into the passing flow of traffic. Jake was expecting Riley to protest, but when he glanced over at her she had her eyes closed. She was white as the tarp that had been covering Gabrielle LeFleuer's body.

"You want to talk about it," he said as he slid over to the fast lane.

"No," she answered through grayish lips that barely moved.

She opened her eyes and turned her head slightly towards him. "But I'm going to have to."

"If we're going to find him."

"I never saw him."

Jake threw a quick glance over at the raw welt of blood caked and swollen tissue encircling her neck. "I know you're hurting, but we need to talk while you still can. In a couple of hours the swelling is going to make it impossible to talk for a day or two."

Riley cocked her left eyebrow at him. "How do you know that?"

Taking his right hand off the steering wheel he tugged his shirt collar down a couple of inches so she could see the faint razor thin scar encircling his own neck.

"Where?"

"Iraq."

Nodding, Riley turned to stare sightlessly out the front window. "The door was open and Gabrielle was on the floor. I started to go help her when he jumped me from behind."

"How did you manage to get away"

Riley gave a weak shake of her head. "I don't know. There was some kind of a metal statue on the chest in the hallway. I used it to stab him until he let go of the noose."

"That explains the fire," Jake said sliding through the fast moving traffic.

"Why?"

"His blood must have splattered on the walls and he needed to destroy that evidence."

Riley tiredly turned her head enough so that she could look at him as they talked. "But it was on the statue too."

Jake shook his head at her. "There wasn't any statue."

"He must have taken it with him, just to be safe," Riley said.

"That makes sense." Jake said as he zipped around a slower moving car.

"I don't understand why you're still alive," Jake said quietly. "Gabrielle was almost completely decapitated."

Riley held up her injured left arm. "This got in the way."

"You were lucky," Jake said quietly.

"I know," Riley said just as softly.

"How did you manage to get away from him?"

"Dumb luck and a dumb waiter," Riley said as she fought to keep her eyes open. The gentle motion of the car and the sunlight warming its interior were both draining her of what little energy she had left.

"What?"

"There was an old dumb waiter shaft. I used it to climb up to the roof."

Jake shook his head in admiration. "Smart woman."

Riley's sudden silence caused Jake to look over at her.

She was slumped towards him sound asleep from exhaustion. Her injured left hand rested lightly against his right thigh. Reaching down he gently squeezed it. "Lucky woman," he whispered so as not to disturb her. Then he turned his attention to the traffic surrounding them.

~~~

Riley came awake with a start.

Jake had just turned off the engine. Confused, she looked around to discover they were in a parking slot at the Port Hercules marina. Glancing through her side window she caught sight of dock after floating dock lined with boats of all lengths, colors and models – from behemoth luxurious ocean-going yachts sporting private helipads, to miniature one-man sailing skiffs.

"Where are we?"

Grasping the key that was still in the ignition, he looked over at her. "The marina," he said pulling the key free and sitting back in his seat to give her time to collect her thoughts.

"The marina? Why?"

Jake looked out through the windshield at the flotilla of boats bobbing on the gentle swell rolling into the harbor. "To keep you out of Moreau's reach."

Riley waited for him to explain.

"Whoever is behind the robbery seems to be making it a point to kill off any potential witnesses," Jake said as he turned to look at her. "And despite the attack on you, I've got a gut feeling that Moreau is going to be picking you up again for more questioning."

"But he doesn't know I was attacked."

Jake gave her a quick smile. "Thanks to Apollo's claim that you whipped his tail in the gym."

Shaking his head, Jake continued. "Sooner or later he's going to get the witness reports from Larson's killing. There were neighbors who saw us there. Then it will only be a matter of time before he'll have a legitimate reason to hold you."

"But I'm out on bail," Riley protested.

"For the Devereux case," Jake pointed out. "Larson's murder is another whole can of worms altogether."

He looked at her. "And you are legally a material witness to that case."

Jake shook his head at her. "And if he ties you to Gabrielle's murder, he'll more than likely throw the entire Napoleonic Code at you.

"Which means," Jake said leaning forward slightly in order to look her in the eye, "he'll find a way to keep you in jail until you are a very, very old woman."

"Great," Riley said shaking her head in frustration as she threw her head back to stare at the ceiling. "I can't win for losing in this town."

Silence filled the space between them as Riley's thoughts swirled in circles in a never-ending game of chase the tail. Waiting patiently to allow her time to come to terms with just how precarious her situation was, Jake studied her face in companionable silence.

She didn't look anything at all like Lily. But like Lily, she had an inner fire that lit up her eyes. And like Lily, he was surprised to admit to himself, for some reason she made him feel alive.

As that realization suddenly flooded through him, Jake turned and looked out the windshield so that Riley couldn't see the sudden flash of surprise that had just hit him.

What was going on with him? Since that terrible day in Madrid, when he arrived at the shattered train station to witness first-hand the carnage that had ripped his world apart, he had been as dead inside as Lily and Katy had been laying broken and torn among the wreckage of the bomb debris.

Katy with her Mum's beautiful dark hair and sky blue eyes. Her four year-old's infectious laughter and gap-tooth smile. Torn from his life by a backpack filled with explosives in the middle of a crowded train of holiday shoppers.

As the razor sharp shards of pain ripped through him, Jake whipped his head around to the driver's side window so that Riley couldn't see him make a fool of himself by going emotional on her. Especially since she didn't have a clue in the world what was going through his mind at this moment. And why should she? She had problems of her own to deal with. Like being a prime suspect in a murder case and directly involved in two other ones on top of that.

Pull yourself together Rafferty, Jake silently chided himself as Riley suddenly stirred in the seat next to him. Pulling down the mask he had been wearing for so long that it had become a permanent feature, Jake casually turned back to find Riley worriedly chewing on her lower lip.

Realizing that he was looking at her, she self-consciously ran her thumb over her bruised lip as she flashed him a weak smile. "Sorry," she said. "It's a bad habit I have."

Turning in her seat to face him, she continued. "I don't understand how I got into this mess. I was just working and minding my own business. And BAM! My world suddenly fell apart. And I don't have a clue why or who is responsible for that."

Looking at the frustration filling her face, Jake wanted to tell her that he knew exactly how she felt. That he understood completely how helpless and confusing it all was. Especially when there wasn't anyone that you could focus your anger and grief at because, whoever he was, he didn't have a face – or a name.

As his own pain and rage echoed back at him, Jake looked at the beautiful woman next to him battered and bruised. She had almost died. Not once but twice.

All because he had used her as bait to draw out an unseen enemy. With disastrous results so far.

But no more.

It was time to take her out of the equation – completely.

Jake shifted slightly in his seat and then he nodded at Riley. "That's why I've decided to stash you somewhere discrete," he said as he opened his door and got out of the car.

Swiftly moving around to Riley's side he opened the door for her. "Here, let me help you," he said as he held out his hand to help her ease out of the low seat. As she turned towards him Jake saw her flinch with pain as she suddenly became aware once more of her injuries.

"If you want, I can take you over to the hospital so they can patch you up," he said as she took his hand and allowed him to ease her out of the car. "Or, we can go for a hot bath and a visit with the medical kit."

Taking a deep breath and straightening her back Riley looked him in the eye. "I'm a nurse. I'm been hurt worst getting thrown by a horse."

Jake grinned at her. "That's the stuff."

Offering her his arm like the proper English gentleman he was, Jake guided her to the gate leading to a nearby floating dock lined with towering luxury yachts.

"Where are we going?" Riley asked him as she stepped through the gate he was holding open for her.

"We're borrowing a client's boat," Jake said as he pulled the gate closed behind him and turned back to her.

Taking her arm he guided her down the ramp to the dock itself. Matching his pace to her slower step he led her to the end of the dock. "Since the boat is in the client's name that should slow Moreau down a bit if he suddenly decides to come looking for you," Jake said they reached a 130" gleaming white yacht two slips from the end of the T-shaped dock.

Taking in its sleek swept-back lines, black wrap-around windows, three-story superstructure and private helipad, Riley shook her head in disbelief.

"You call this 'discreet'?" she said.

CAROL A. HUGHES

CHAPTER 21

She looked up at him as she continued, "I suppose to you Buckingham Palace is just a little shack by the river."

Jake laughed at her mocking tone.

"What does your client do for a living?" she asked him.

Guiding her towards the metal steps leading up to the main deck he said, "He's a Sheik."

"A Sheik?"

"Yes," Jake said nonchalantly as he followed her up the steps.

"Okay," she said matching his nonchalant tone as they reached the main deck and he led her into the main salon. She didn't know what she had been expecting, but what she found was pleasantly surprising. Sleek modern lines, polished teakwood accents, recessed lights, sparkling glass shelves and mirrored recesses reflected the warm hues of the setting sunlight filling the room.

"It's beautiful," she said taking in the understated elegance surrounding her.

"More importantly," Jake said moving past her towards a lobby visible beyond the salon's interior glass doors, "it's private."

"And discrete," Riley added with a smile tugging at the corner of her mouth.

Catching the twinkle of humor in her tired eyes, Jake returned her amused smile. "Definitely discrete."

He beckoned to her to follow him as he continued on towards the airy, white marble-lined lobby. "Let's get you settled in and patched up."

Following him into the lobby's gilded elevator, Riley got her first real look at herself in the elevator's mirrored walls. She was covered in stains and dried blood from head to toe. Her hair was a mare's nest of tangles. The dark circles under her eyes looked like smudge bruises. Her poor throat was swollen to almost three times its normal size. And the sight of the raw welt of torn flesh encircling the center of her throat made her want to cry.

She felt like a horse that had been run hard and put away wet.

Catching the look of shocked dismay flitting across her face Jake said softly, "It'll heal."

As she blinked back tears, he continued encouragingly, "What's important is that you are still alive. That's all that really matters."

Reaching the stateroom level, Jake paused as the elevator door opened to reveal a thickly carpeted long corridor paralleling the window-lined starboard side of the ship. "What you need to focus on is our catching the bastard and whoever else is involved," Jake said as he gestured for her to exit.

Giving him a fleeting smile of thanks, Riley nodded as she gathered her resolve and stepped out into the silent corridor. Following her out of the elevator, Jake led her to the rear of the ship and the three room master suite with its own private sundeck visible through the darkened glass doors lining the suite's sitting area.

As luxurious and modern as the salon on the deck above, Riley took in the champagne colored suite with neutral toned upholstered chairs and love seat filling the sitting area. Brightly colored abstracts hung from the textured walls and cheerfully colored accent pillows on the furniture added bright splashes of much welcomed color to the room's palette.

To her left two steps led up to the large sleeping area with its over-sized bed flanked by a recessed wet bar lined with lighted frosted glass panels and sparkling stemware. Spotting it, Riley arched an inquisitive eyebrow at Jake. "Your friend drinks?"

"Never when he's home."

Stepping up to the bedroom area, Riley discovered the third room that jutted out towards the rear sundeck, was a marble-lined, glass-walled fantasy bathroom with its own private enclosed patio containing a Jacuzzi that could easily hold six people. Seeing her cocking an eyebrow at the sight of it, Jake shrugged as he told her, "The client is rather hefty."

"That explains the size of the bed then," she said as she turned and led him back to the sleeping area.

Jake indicated a door on the opposite wall. "That's a walk-in closet where you'll find a collection of women's clothing."

Again Riley cocked an eyebrow at him in query.

"He's got a few wives. Some of them are your size."

"How many?"

Jake had the decency to blush. "Ten or so."

"Ten?"

When Jake shifted uncomfortably, Riley laughed and shook her head at him. "Busy man."

Anxious to change the topic, Jake caught Riley off-guard when he crossed the room to a burled walnut built-in dresser lined with groupings of fragrant candles. In fact, when Riley looked around the room she realized that there were groupings of candles scattered all around the entire suite.

Well with ten wives, Riley thought to herself, the Sheik was either a hopeless romantic, or a smooth operator.

As Jake opened a drawer and began searching through its contents, Riley asked him, "What are you looking for?"

"This," he answered as he turned around and held up a long tapered candle lighter.

As he began moving around the room lighting candles, he casually called over his shoulder to her. "I don't want you to get the wrong idea here," he said.

"Oh?"

Finished with the sleeping area candles, Jake moved down to the sitting area and continued on with his self-appointed task as Riley watched him warily from her position by the open bathroom door.

"So you're lighting candles because . . .?" she said warily.

Finished lighting the last of the candles, he laid the lighter on the glass coffee table anchoring the seating area. Looking over at her as he moved towards the suite's hallway door, he paused long enough to say quietly, "With the day you've had I thought that maybe you'd prefer candlelight to harsh lighting."

As the thoughtfulness of his gesture hit home, Riley found herself fighting to swallow around the lump in her throat that had nothing to do with her injury.

Seeing her rapidly blinking back unexpected tears, Jake had the decency to glance away. "There's a decent medical kit under the bathroom sink." While you're cleaning up, I'm going to check out the mess and see what kind of a dinner I can pull together for us.

"You can cook too?" Riley joked as she sniffed away her unshed tears.

"I can at least scramble eggs and make toast, if nothing else." Jack said banteringly as he headed out the door. "How's thirty minutes sound?"

"Fine," Riley answered. "Now that you brought up the subject of food, I just realized that I'm starving."

With a quick nod Jake disappeared out the door and Riley headed for the closet to see what she could find in the way of a fresh set of clothes.

~~~

Returning thirty minutes later with a tray containing two covered dinner plates, a steaming pot of fresh tea, and two mugs to share with Riley, Jake rapped smartly on the suite door.

Faintly through the heavy teak doors he heard a muffled "come in."

I don't like the sound of that, he thought as he maneuvered the food tray through the open door.

"Dinner is served," he called out cheerily as he crossed the sitting area and placed the tray on the glass coffee table.

When he was met with silence he turned and scanned the shadowy sleeping area for a sign of Riley. He found her hidden in the flickering candle light huddled back against the bed's headboard.

185

"Riley, are you all right," he said softly as he cautiously moved towards her.

Reaching the end of the bed he paused to give her time to adjust to his presence. From the haunted look in her eyes he realized that she had come off of the adrenaline high that had saved her life. And that she was now slipping into shock as the cacophony of today's events finally began to really sink in for her.

"It's okay," he said softly to her. "You're safe here. Nobody knows you're here."

He had slipped his jacket off and rolled up his shirt sleeves while he was making dinner for them. But he had left on his shoulder rig so that his gun was near at hand. Patting it lightly with his right hand to reassure her, he continued. "I promise you that whoever they are, they aren't going to hurt you ever again."

Riley had found a lavender pair of velour hip hugging pants and a silky white short top with a scooped neck that nicely showed off her sculpted lean waist and the soft swell of her breast. Upon discovering the drawers of lacey bras and dainty thongs she felt like she had fallen into Victoria's own Secret world.

Soaking in the fragranced warmth of a decadent bubble bath, she let her imagination loose for the first time ever. In the soft glow of the flickering candlelight, she had carte blanche to explore her own secret fantasy of being secluded on a yacht luxurious beyond her wildest imaginings. With a sexy British hunk and wearing the most scandalous undergarments she ever thought possible.

Lulled by the warmth of the water cradling her she had dozed off. How long she slept she couldn't tell. Long enough for her bathwater to chill. When she found herself dreaming, she was in a sunny meadow of wildflowers. Turning to look around, she spotted a smiling Jake opening his arms to welcome her. She laughed and ran towards him.

But as she got closer, the view around her twisted like a TV picture suddenly twisting on the screen. And the man waiting for her wasn't Jake anymore. Instead it was a dark-haired man wearing black leather gloves and holding the ends of a wire garrote in his hands. As he leered murderously at her, Riley opened her mouth to scream, but her throat was on fire and no sound would come out of her mouth.

She couldn't breathe and the leering man started moving towards her like a panther stalking its prey. She wanted to run, but when she tried it seemed as though she was running in place and the killer was coming closer and closer.

Just as he reached out to drop the wire loop over her head, Riley woke with a start that jerked her upright in the tub of bathwater. The water had chilled only slightly, but Riley was suddenly freezing and shaking with chills that seemed to be radiating out from deep inside of her.

Heaving herself out of the deep onyx tub with a cry, she collapsed in a heap when her rubbery legs refused to support her. With her racing heart sending her blood thundering in her ears, Riley forced herself to pull in deep calming breaths as she admonished herself. Get it together nurse Copper. This is no time for you to fall apart like some hysterical virgin. You're safe. You're alive. Jake Rafferty is here and whoever they are they are going to have to come through him to get to you. So get your act together and stop acting like you don't know what an adrenaline crash is. You're a nurse for heaven's sake.

Straightening her spine and lifting her chin in defiance, Riley willed herself to climb up off of the marble floor and stand up straight. *What do you do when you get thrown?* She could hear her Dad's words echoing in her mind. *You climb back on and show him who's the boss.* She heard her young girl's voice ring out in her memory.

Using the palm of her hand to wipe the moisture off of the mirror over the sink, Riley stared at the hollow-eyed woman in the mirror. And as much as it pained her, she had to admit that the sight of that woman's haunted eyes frightened her more than the memory of the attack itself.

Would the terror she felt as she fought for her life always be there from now on? Would she never be free from it? How was she going to go on like this if she didn't find her lost courage again?

Those were the thoughts tumbling through her mind as Jake carefully eased around the end of the bed she was now huddled on like a frightened child. Give her time and the shakes would disappear the charge nurse in her whispered in her inner ear. But for now she felt like she was never going to get warm again. And how could she fight back against the bastard who did this to her if she couldn't stop shaking like a newborn calf trying to get to its feet for the very first time.

"Jake," she called softly from the bed. "I'm know I'm safe here. But I keep seeing him when I close my eyes."

She shuddered involuntarily, "And I keep feeling him pressing against me. Choking me."

She looked at him with haunted eyes. "He keeps reaching for me. And if I fall asleep, I'm afraid he's going to get me."

She shook her head. "I know it's stupid. But…"

Letting out a shuddering breath, she slowly ran her tongue over suddenly parched lips. Then she closed her eyes to steel herself against his gaze. "Would you hold me?

Even in the soft glow of the fluttering candle light he could see her throat work as she swallowed. "Just…," she hesitated, and then blinked as a sheen of moisture unexpectedly threatening to spill over her lashes. "Just until I fall asleep."

The torment in her eyes silenced any doubts he had about keeping her at arm's length – at least for tonight. Lily forgive me he silently intoned as he nodded slowly and quietly unsnapped his shoulder rig.

Never taking his eyes off of her face he eased out of the rig. The relief filling her eyes hitched his breath as he dropped the holster and gun on the barrel chair at the foot of the bed.

"Thank you," she whispered as she slid down on her side to watch him slip off his shoes and cross over to her. A wan smile touched her lips as he gently eased down beside her on the bed.

"I know it's silly but …," she started to say.

"Shh," he whispered. "I'm here."

Sighing from the depths of her soul, Riley slowly nodded her head as her eyes fluttered shut and her lashes brushed her checks like butterfly kisses.

"Come here," he said softly as he reached out to enfold her in his arms. "You're safe now."

Pulling her close, he could feel the tension beneath her soft skin. And her heart was beating like a caged bird against her chest. "Shh," he said into the softness of her hair. "It's going to be all right."

He was content just to feel her warm skin against his own. And to hear her jagged breathing slow to a gentle lull as she began to relax against the length of him. Breathing in the fragrance of her hair he suddenly remembered a sunlit afternoon by the river with Lily dozing gently in the warm summer breezes. He remembered how those breezes carried the faint scent of summer roses and lavender through the air around them.

It had been so long since he last held a woman in his arms. And now he was like a man lost in the desert for years who was unexpectedly encountering his first spring rain. He wanted to drink up every scent and feel of her. The soft brush of her breasts against his chest. The warmth of her being filling all of the cold and lonely crevices of his heart.

As if she was of one mind with him, Riley melted against the contours of his body with a soft sigh of contentment. Like a lost kitten, she nuzzled against him and felt his swelling erection brush lightly against her. Sensing her awareness, he tried to ease back but a soft sigh slipped naturally through her lips.

"Don't," she breathed into the curve of his neck. "I want ...," she whispered as she turned her face towards his and opened her lips to him. Her lips were hot on his as her tongue began to probe between his lips.

He hesitated for a moment, then pulled her forward and lost himself in the taste and feel of her mouth. Probing, tasting, touching, he explored the soft moistness of her as his hands shaped the outline of her body with feather-light caresses.

Slipping his hands up under her top, his fingertips lightly stroked her velvety skin, sending waves of sensations radiating through her like ripples in a still lake. As he slowly rubbed the silk lace of her bra covering her nipples, Riley moaned softly and lifted her leg to rest on top of his thigh in order to press against his rock hard erection.

Skimming her top over her willing arms Jake gently lowered his mouth to the soft swell of her breasts and lightly ran the tip of his tongue along the lacey edge of her bra. Arching her back to meet the warm sensation of his touch, Riley moaned in contentment as her nipples pebbled in anticipation.

"Please," she whispered as soft as that long ago summer breeze as he tenderly removed a breast from its lacey confines and slowly ran the tip of his tongue around the base of her throbbing nipple. "Yes," she moaned thrusting into his willing mouth.

As he lightly trailed his fingers beneath the edge of her panties, Riley lost herself to the waves of sensations throbbing through her as he lightly suckled her breast. Gently at first he took her into his mouth and ran his tongue back and forth over her nipple. With each pass it throbbed in anticipation. All the while he continued to suckle her faster and deeper as he filled his mouth with the taste and feel of her.

At the same time, his fingers softly delved into her wetness and gently parted her lips to slide across the aching length of her as she rose up to meet his touch. Reaching the heart of her moistness, he slowly slid two fingers into her throbbing heat and sent a flood of sensations racing up the core of her.

She moaned as waves of ecstasy radiated out from the center of her soul. Faster and faster he stroked. Setting her blood on fire and sending warm heat seeping through her, loosening tight muscles and enveloping her in a sense of security like she had never known before.

His wet, slick fingers thrust deeper and deeper into her with each stroke as she moved against him, moaning softly with each penetration. Faster and faster, deeper and deeper he thrust until she cried out as the first convulsion ripped through her. Shuddering in complete release, Riley wound her arms around his neck and thrust against his hand.

"More," she breathed in his ear. "I want all of you in me now."

Clamping her warm muscles around his fingers to hold him fast, Riley opened her mouth to suck in his tongue while her fingers freed the length of him against her bare skin. Grasping his erection gently in her hands, she skimmed her fingers along his length as he groaned softly into her mouth.

Rocking gently against his trapped fingers she released them and guided him into her as she rose to meet him.

Pulsing and hot, Jake pushed into her as she moved against him, moaning softly. "Yes, yes, yes," she urged him on.

He intended to take things slow, but she drove the pace by meeting each of his thrusts with her throbbing embrace until he lost himself completely in the warmth of her wetness and rocking thrusts. Faster and faster he stroked as she threw back her head and gave herself to him all over again. He thrust deeper and deeper, harder and harder, again and again and again until they both reached the peak at the same moment and balanced on the knife edge of ecstasy and awe.

Her fingers curled in his hair and she began to writhe beneath him as the first spasm hit her. She cried out in joy as spasm after spasm coursed through her. Tearing her loose from heaven and earth and sending her whirling to the outer reaches of the cosmos as his heat flooded through her.

As Riley throbbed around the length of his shaft Jake felt his own release cresting as wave after wave of sensation smashed through him in a tsunami of fire gushing out of him to fill all of her warm places.

Collapsing on top of her, he gulped in draughts of cool air as his heart beat slowly dropped out of the stratosphere. Rolling onto his back, he wrapped his arms around her and pulled Riley willingly onto his chest.

When he could finally speak, he looked her in the eye and simply said, "Wow."

Smiling lazily at him like a contented cat, she said. "Let's do that again."

He laughed at the grin on her face. "I don't think...," he started to protest. But her fingers stroking him made an instant liar out of him.

Their first time had been hard and fast.

The second was lazy and slow.

The third time was perfection itself.

By the time they were ready to go yet again, dawn was daintily lifting her skirt hem and the terror was a distant memory in Riley's mind.

CHAPTER 22

Rising slowly through the layers of sleep, Riley felt a lightness of spirit that she had never felt before. With her eyes still closed she rolled gently over on her side so that the first thing she would see when she opened them would be Jake's face.

Smiling in anticipation of that sight she slowly opened them – to an empty bed.

Clutching the silk sheet to her breast as she rose up on her elbow to look for him in the sitting area, the silence told her she was completely alone in the suite. A tendril of unease edged under her breastbone until her eyes swept across the surface of the bedside clock.

It was 10:37 and sunlight was flooding in through the surrounding windows.

Smiling to herself, Riley laid back on her pillow and laughed softly. Never in all of her life had she slept in this late. Not even after pulling double shifts in the ER. But then again she had never made love all night long with a lover as incredible as Jake Rafferty had been.

The man absolutely wore her out.

He had been insatiable. But then again, so had she.

And she couldn't wait to do it all over again.

As that thought ballooned through her mind, Riley shook her head at her newly discovered wantonness. Now where in the world did that come from she wondered as she contentedly looked around her. If she hadn't experienced last night for herself, she would never have believed that she had it in her to be so open. Or so sensual.

Especially not when she was lying on the bathroom floor shivering from fear.

Fear!

The memory jolted her upright in bed.

Not fear she thought as she scrambled out of bed and grabbed her discarded clothing off of the floor. Terror.

Downright pure terror.

Terror like she had never known before. Not even in the midst of any of the deadliest combat situations she had experienced during her three back-to-back combat tours in Osama bin Laden's former backyard playground.

OBL was dead and she would be too if she didn't do something to gain the upper hand. And take back the control of her life that had been steadily ripped away from her, starting with the collapse of her marriage.

Hurrying into the nearby bathroom to grab a quick shower, Riley's mind was racing at the speed of light as it clicked through the various scenarios and options available to her at the moment.

Talking to Jake and convincing him that they would have a better chance of unraveling the mystery behind the attack that started the whole mess she was currently in was her first order of business. As she hurried across the room and into the bathroom, it felt good to find herself once again rock steady and with a definite goal in mind. Since the disaster of her marriage falling apart and revealing the depths of her husband's betrayal, Riley had been shell-shocked and drifting without a purpose to anchor her to solid ground.

Now she had one.

Fighting to prove her innocence.

Fighting for justice for her two dead companions.

Try as she might, she just couldn't factor Bill Larson into that equation. Maybe because she had never considered him to be anything more than a slightly irritating co-worker. Then there was his convenient alibi provided by a professional call girl who made more in one night that Bill earned in one year.

She didn't have the faintest clue how Bill Larson and Gabrielle LeFleuer tied into the attack on the penthouse. But they were both dead. And even though the murder weapons were completely different, the use of fire to destroy the evidence seemed to link their deaths to Étienne Devereux's and Carmela Paulino's.

Three separate fires and three separate murder sites. They had to be tied in some way. But how? And why?

That was what she needed to find out.

Reaching the shower, she opened the glass shower door and turned on the spray nozzle. As she adjusted the flow, she thought about Étienne Devereux. He had turned into an unexpected friend and had provided her with a temporary safe harbor. But that had been ripped away from her with his murder.

As the shower water heated up, Riley continued to look inward. She had survived her ex. And she had survived war. Now she had survived someone trying to kill her.

Not once but three separate times.

Enough was enough.

They picked the wrong cowgirl to mess with she thought as she stepped into the steaming shower and closed the glass door behind her.

CHAPTER 23

Alone in the shower you can be as brave as a comic book superhero, Riley thought as she rode the elevator up to the ship's lobby. Now it was time to separate the chickens from the chicks and find out if she really did have what she needed to get the job done the way she needed it done.

And the first step was going to be the hardest.

Facing Jake and the others with nothing standing between her and them.

The makeup she found in the bathroom didn't match her skin tone. So she had no other choice but to face the world without the protection of any makeup at all except for a light dusting of jewel-toned eye shadow and a quick swipe of clear lip gloss. Not that she was a makeup maven by any stretch of the imagination. Foolish or not, she had definitely earned the right to display the tapestry of cuts and bruises from her encounter with her would-be killer yesterday.

On the other hand, the accompanying whisker burns were not intended for public display or discussion. Yet here she was – barefaced to the world - and her very private business now out there for every one of Jake's colleagues to see with their own eyes.

Reaching the lobby and stepping out of the elevator, Riley paused for a moment to blow out a couple of deep breaths before determinedly entering the salon and facing the consequences of last night.

The moment she stepped into the room it was instantly clear to her that Jake and his team had been hard at work for hours. Yesterday's display salon was now a beehive of activity and a warren of high tech gear spilled over tables and countertops. She guessed that encrypted laptops and cell phones worked just as well on board a $100 million luxury yacht as they did back at their home base. And that the Internet was an equal opportunity distributor of information no matter where a terminal was located.

Glancing around further she spotted a tall silver coffee urn sitting on the side bar surrounded by a collection of coffee mugs and sweet rolls. Max and Apollo were camped out on opposite ends of one of the couches working on their laptops. Derrick had commandeered one of the Louis XIVth tables and Jake and Claudine had their heads together discussing whatever was on her monitor. Based on the tired looks on their faces, she had no problems figuring out that the first the results of their efforts had been disappointing.

Nervously, she waited for someone to notice her and say something. But aside from a quick nod from Max who spotted when he glanced up from his monitor, Jake and the others never paused in what they were doing. Too nervous to stomach coffee at the moment, Riley gathered her resolve and crossed over to join Jake and Claudine.

"You really didn't expect it to surface this quickly, did you?" Riley heard Claudine say to Jake as she walked up to them.

Seeing Riley for the first time, Claudine smiled at her. "How are you doing this morning?"

Jake straightened up from where he had been resting one hand on the back of Claudine's chair, and the other on the edge of her desk, as he had stood bent over watching the data streaming across her monitor along with her.

"I'm fine," Riley replied to Claudine as she felt the weight of Jake's silent stare.

"I need to talk to you," she said turning to Jake.

Jake straightened to his full height and took a step back from her. "Can it wait?" he said as he crossed his arm in front of him. "We're in the middle of a few things at the moment."

Riley didn't have to look around to know that every eye in the place was focused directly on her and Jake.

And it was clear from the expressions on everyone's face that they were as puzzled by Jake's cool reception as she was.

Shifting uncomfortably in her chair, Claudine started to rise as Riley turned back to Jake with sparks of anger starting to flare in her eyes. "Why don't I go get a cup of coffee and let you two talk?" Claudine said as she got up to move.

"You don't have to leave," Riley told her as she locked eyes with Jake. "I just want to say," she continued loud enough for everyone to hear her. "That I want to help anyway I can."

Riley caught the tiniest flicker of relief in Jake's eyes before he shuttered his emotions. And that only served to spike the sudden anger that flared in her own eyes as she looked back at him.

"I realized this morning that I acted like a fool yesterday," she said carefully enunciating each word. Turning away from Jake, Riley continued to Claudine. "I never should have tried to talk to Gabrielle on my own."

"We all make mistakes," Claudine told her. "The objective is to learn from them."

Swinging her gaze back at Jake, Riley nodded her head in reply as she said, "I couldn't agree more."

"What are you proposing?" Jake asked cautiously.

This time it was Riley who took the step back and crossed her arms before speaking. "To do whatever it takes to prove that I had nothing at all to do with Étienne Devereux's death or the disappearance of Constanza's necklace."

Being so close to them Claudine could almost physically feel the tension as it crackled between the two of them. Like the others, she had a pretty good idea how Riley and Jake had spent the evening. That was great as far as she was concerned. Because it was about time that Jake finally started living again. Although she didn't know Jake at the time, she had come to learn all of the tragic details about the death of his wife and little girl when a group of terrorist had blown up the Madrid train station.

He and Derrick had been working for MI6 then. And he was in Madrid attending an International Anti-Terrorist Conference when the attack took place. Since he and his family were planning on spending a few days vacationing on the Costa Brava after the conference was over, they were all in Madrid together that week.

And like Derrick and the others, she knew that Jake blamed himself for their deaths. Even though there hadn't been even the slightest rumor of a planned attack prior to the bombs going off in all of those packed early morning commuter trains.

It was fate that killed them. Not Jake's incompetence as an agent.

She and the others had tried to tell him that ever since then. But for Jake his life ended the second Lily and Katy died. Since then he had merely been going through the motions of getting on with his life.

As far as she was personally concerned, if Jake did sleep with Riley then good for the both of them. Because Riley was the first woman since Lily he had even looked at in that way. And *Dieu* knew that everyone deserves a little romance in their life. Even tough as steel Jake Rafferty.

To keep from saying something to Jake that she might regret later on, Riley paused to look around the room at Derrick and the others. Turning back to Jake and Claudine, Riley said, "I'm going to take a minute to get a cup of coffee. Then you can tell me what I can do to help out here."

Before either of them could reply, Riley turned and walked away.

Jake Rafferty may think he was running the show she thought as she crossed the room. And he may have saved her life – twice. And he may have slept with her. OK, she may have slept with him. But that did not mean that he was going to run her life. She knew how do to research on the Internet. All right, maybe not exactly like he and his people did. But she was as smart as any of them. And she had as much chance of figuring out who wanted to harm Étienne as they did.

Arriving at the coffee urn, Riley grabbed an empty mug and began to fill it. As she did she gave herself a mental shake. Who do you think you're kidding, she asked herself. What you're really upset about is the fact that once again you blew it when it came to choosing a man.

Reaching for the bowl of sugar and a spoon she continued with her internal monologue. Why is it that you always go for the tall, dark, handsome ones whose only interest in you is what they can get from you. Mark used you to get control of the Double H. And Jake used you as bait to draw out a killer. And then he pretended that he cared about you just so he could sleep with you. Riley could feel her blood pressure building as the anger inside of her bubbled higher and higher.

"Is that really how much you want?" a voice said from behind her, intruding into her thoughts.

"What...?" Looking up from the spoon of sugar in her hand Riley found Derrick staring at her thoughtfully.

"Do you normally drink a little coffee with your sugar, like that?" he said pointing to the spoon of sugar she was about to dump into her cup. "I figured that after the sixth teaspoon that maybe you were a little distracted. So I thought that maybe I should check on you to see if there was anything I could do to help?"

Picking up her cup of coffee off of the counter, Derrick walked around the bar counter and dumped its contents into the bar sink. He avoided looking at Riley so that she could have time to recover from the blush that was coloring her cheeks. Watching the coffee disappear down the sink drain he said to her, "He's really not a bad guy. Once you get to know him."

Grabbing another empty mug, Riley busied herself with filling it as Derrick returned to her side of the counter. Heading back to his desk he said, "Be careful on the sugar."

Glancing back in Jake's direction she found him scrutinizing her while Claudine worked forgotten by his side. Turning away to pour some cream into her black coffee, Riley told herself, OK he's been using you. So now it's your turn to return the favor. Two can play the same game.

Pasting a determinedly neutral look on her face. Riley straightened her shoulders, turned around, and marched back over to Jake and Claudine with her fresh cup of coffee in hand.

"OK," she said when she reached them. "Where do we start?"

Shooting a quick look over Riley's shoulder, Jake saw both Apollo and Max watching him like a pair of hawks. Derrick returned his look by giving him the slightest of nods signaling his approval.

Shifting his gaze back to Riley, he saw the spark of determination in her eye and the stubborn set of her chin. That alone made him want to take her into his arms again and drag her back to bed. But he had a job to do. And that meant that he needed to keep her at arms' length for her own good. And his sanity.

Claudine glanced up at Jake when he didn't immediately respond. Rolling her eyes at the stubbornness of some men, she turned back to Riley and said, "So far there hasn't been so much as a whisper in the black market about the Constanza Necklace."

Riley frowned thoughtfully as she said, "Did you really expect it would show up this early?"

"You never know," Claudine said with a typical Gallic shrug. "It's possible that it's currently being re-cut in order to mask its identity."

"It's also possible that whoever took it is too busy killing potential witnesses to be dealing with the necklace right now," Riley said.

Despite himself, Jake had to admit that Riley made an excellent point. Reluctantly he forced himself to say, "That might explain the rocket attack on us."

As Apollo and the others joined them, he continued. "They were trying to silence you along with Larson and Gabrielle."

"You're either the luckiest woman alive," Max said. "Or else you've got more lives than a cat."

"Three attacks in three days tells us that whoever they are, they are very determined to cover their tracks," Derrick said to the group.

"Something doesn't feel right," Riley said as a frown tugged a parallel furrow between her eyebrows.

"What doesn't feel right?" Jake asked genuinely curious.

Riley looked over at him. "Killing Bill and Gabrielle I can understand," she said. "Because they knew the identity of at least one person involved. Maybe even everybody's identity."

She glanced around at the others and gave them a slight shake of her head. "But I don't know anything. So why kill me? I can't identify anybody."

"Except Gabrielle's killer," Claudine said.

"No," Riley told her. "I never got a look at his face. I wouldn't know him if he walked up to me."

"He doesn't know that," Apollo said.

"Which makes you a liability to him and whoever he's working with," Jake told her.

"So you think that more than one person was involved?" Riley asked him as she looked him in the eye.

Returning her look Jake nodded at her. "Larson and Gabrielle were killed for a reason."

"Maybe the guy didn't want to share the loot with them," Riley suggested.

"Maybe," Jake admitted. "But if you never saw him during the attack on the Penthouse..."

"I didn't," Riley interrupted him.

Nodding at her, Jake continued his train of thought, "Then why try to kill you at Larson's place?"

Riley considers his question.

"At that point you couldn't identify him. And you were unconscious when he was inside the Penthouse. So you were no danger to him then."

"Especially since he thought she was going to die in the fire along with the others," Claudine said.

"Attacking you at Gabrielle's makes sense," Derrick said. "Since he was afraid that you might be able to identify him there."

Riley nodded her head in agreement. "But I still don't see why you think that more than one person was involved."

"Experience," Apollo answered.

Riley gives them a surprised look. "Are you telling me that you've robbed a place before?"

Max laughed and shook his head at her.

"No," Jake said lightly. "But we've definitely infiltrated high security areas before. So we know what it takes to get in and out in a minimum of time and still not leave any evidence of our visit behind."

"That takes teamwork," Derrick said. "And precision."

"And the weapons," Apollo said.

"What about them?" Riley asked him.

"Your average jewel theft likes to get in and out without anyone even knowing that they've been there," Claudine said. "So they usually try to avoid any contact whatsoever with the targeted victim."

Riley nodded in understanding.

"If they hit a place like a jewelry store, they don't usually use a rocket launcher as a weapon," she continued.

"And a garrote is a covert weapon," Max said.

"Not something you usually see a thief use to kill a victim," Claudine said.

Again, Riley slowly nodded her head at them. "So you think that whoever is involved has a military background?"

Jake and the others nod at her.

Once again she looks over at Jake. "And you think it was a team who hit the Penthouse, not just one man?"

"Yes. It had all the hallmarks of a commando raid."

"OK," Riley said. "I can buy that."

Behind her Apollo and Max exchanged approving looks.

"And whoever was involved, seems to have known Étienne," she said. "Or at least was familiar enough with him to know there was a paste copy of Constanza's necklace floating around."

"And knew that Constanza was wearing it the night of the fire," Claudine said.

"But how did they know?" Riley asked looking around at the group.

"Larson told them." Max said. "It's pretty clear he was their inside man."

Frowning, Riley shook her head at him. "He wouldn't have know that."

"What do you mean?" Jake asked her. "He was there when Constanza left for the Palace."

Riley still shook her head at him. "Constanza really didn't like Bill. I never heard her exchange a single word with him the entire six months I worked there. And he was definitely intimidated by her."

Jake and the others wait for her to continue.

"There's no way he could have possibly known that she was wearing the paste copy that night," Riley said looking back at them.

"Unless she told him," Claudine said excitedly.

"Which, I can guarantee you, she wouldn't have," Riley told.

"So how did he know?" Derrick asked the question they were all thinking.

"He didn't," Apollo said as he mulled over this new puzzle.

"That means that somebody else did," Jake said quietly.

"Somebody who was with Constanza that evening," Riley said.

From the looks being passed around her, Riley knew that the others agreed with her. And that made her feel good. It made her feel like she belonged. And that they had accepted her – even Jake. At least as temporarily part of the team.

Then a slight frown skipped across her face. "But it still doesn't make any sense," she said to Jake and the others.

"What doesn't?" Jake asked her.

"The necklace," she said.

"What about it?" Derrick asked.

Riley looked over at him. "OK, it's worth $157 million."

Derrick nodded for her to continue.

She looked over at Jake. "Étienne was worth billions."

Jake nodded at her.

"Why didn't they grab him for ransom? Why did they just leave him there to die and just walk away with the trinket?"

"Some trinket," Max muttered.

"No, wait a minute," Claudine said watching Riley's face very carefully. "She's right." Claudine looked around at her teammates. "Why didn't they snatch him for the ransom?"

"Because he was supposed to die in that fire," Riley said quietly.

"Just like you and Carmela," Apollo added.

Riley shook her at head at him. "I don't think so. I think we were merely collateral damage."

She turned to Jake as she continued, "We were there just to mask the real target of that attack."

CHAPTER 24

Jake returned Riley's unwavering stare.

She was the first to see the realization flood his eyes.

"I think you're right," he admitted. "Especially if the team that went in there was as STRAK as it appears."

"'STRAK'?" Claudine said.

"It's military slang for having your act together," Riley said looking over at her. "Of being top-notched."

At that moment Max's computer pinged him.

Hurrying across the room to check on the waiting message, he called over his shoulder, "Hang on. I've got incoming."

"Fire or a message?" Apollo joked with him.

Riley saw the puzzled look on Claudine's face. "Artillery fire," she explained.

Claudine shook her head in response. "Why don't they just speak English when they are speaking English?"

Riley laughed with her as Max returned with the sheaf paper he had just pulled off of his printer.

"You guys are going to love this," he said as he handed the page to Jake to read.

"What is it?" Apollo said.

"Gabrielle wasn't French," Jake replied as he continued to read the information on the page.

"What was she?" Riley asked.

Jake looked up at her. "Russian," he said. "Her real name was Olga Smalyaninova."

"She was Russian?" Apollo said looking between Jake and Max.

Claudia said softly to Riley. "No wonder she changed her name."

"And that's not all," Max said grinning back at Apollo.

Jake locked eyes with Derrick as he said, "She was KGB."

"Interesting," Derrick replied thoughtfully.

Riley looked back and forth between them. "I thought the KGB went out of business when the Soviet Union collapsed."

"No," Claudine said to her. "They just changed their name and started a whole new line of business."

"What are they now?" Riley asked.

"The Russian Mafia," Jake told her.

"Common criminals?"

"Run by former KGB agents," Derrick said.

"There's nothing 'former' about them," Jake said to Derrick.

"True." Derrick agreed.

"Does Monaco have a problem with the Russian Mafia?" Riley asked.

"No," Claudine told her. "They just bank their billions here."

"Not just here," Derrick said.

"And they're not the only shady characters who bank here," Max said. "You've got arms dealers and the drug cartels banking here too."

"That's not unique to Monaco," Riley said. "Every major bank in just about every major country is used to launder illicit business funds. That's what feeds the world's money supplies and keeps money in circulation."

"I didn't realize you were a banking expert," Jake said.

Riley shot him an irritated look. "I'm not. But Étienne Devereux was. And his passion was international banking. So what else was he going to talk about during his physical therapy sessions?"

Stepping in to tamp down the sudden spark of tension between the two of them, Derrick said soothingly, "That must have made for some interesting therapy sessions for you."

Breaking off eye contact with Jake, she looked over at Derrick. "I'd call them educational. It certainly explained how Étienne made his billions."

She turned back to Jake. "And that's one of the reasons why he was doing business with Alexei Zhukov."

"Meaning?" Jake said.

"Meaning that before he became an oil billionaire, Alexei Zhukov was a KGB Colonel."

"How do you know that?" Jake demanded as he threw a piercing look over at Derrick, who was caught as off-guard as he was that Riley knew about Alexei Zhukov.

"Étienne told me," she said returning his penetrating stare. "Étienne liked to talk about all of the interesting people he knew. . . . A lot."

Once again Derrick stepped in to diffuse the tension between them by saying to Jake, "So Gabrielle was still working for Zhukov after all."

Before Jake could respond to Derrick, Riley said to him. "You already knew. Didn't you?"

She read the answer on his face.

Turning to Derrick she said, "What do you mean that Gabrielle was working for Zhukov?"

"Alexei Zhukov likes to party when he's here," Derrick answered her. "And Gabrielle was always present at all of his parties."

"On the arm of her 'friend' for the night." Claudine noted.

"But what she was really doing was collecting intelligence for him," Riley said. "Well that explains the permanent source of her income. And the escort service would give her a perfect cover."

"And mask the real source of her income." Derrick said.

"No wonder the cops never could bust her for prostitution," Apollo said shaking his head in admiration.

"Did she ever try to hook up with you?" Riley unexpectedly asked Jake.

"Me?" Jake said caught off guard by her question.

"Sure? With clients like Étienne you could provide her with all kinds of valuable insider information that she and Zhukov could have used."

"I don't date call girls," Jake said icily. "And I never discuss my clients. With anyone."

Riley arched an eyebrow at him. "That's good to know."

Quietly fuming, Jake started to turn away but Riley wasn't done with him yet.

"You never did answer the question," she said. "Did Gabrielle, or Olga, or whatever her name was, try to hook up with you?

Jake's eyes blazed at her and his lips pressed into a razor thin line before he answered. "Yes."

"And?"

"And I turned her down," Jake shot out at her through stiff lips.

Riley just couldn't help herself. "Because you don't date call girls."

As an uncomfortable silence grows between them, Claudine broke the growing tension by asking, "So are we saying that the KGB killed Étienne Devereux?"

Snapping his attention away from Riley, Jake turned to Claudine. "No. But it does explain a lot of things."

"Yeah," Apollo said. "Like how they got a rocket launcher into Monaco."

It may have been childish, but Riley felt better for venting her anger at Jake by bringing up Gabrielle like that.

But as much as she hated to do it, she was going to have to face the fact that she was the one who had invited him into her bed to begin with. In fact, putting it that way, she realized that who she was really angry at was herself – not Jake.

And to be brutally honest with herself, she was the one who choose to ask him to hold her to keep the boogeyman at bay. So why in the world was she mad at him for giving her the most incredible night of her entire life?

Honestly, how stupid was that? No wonder Mark was able to con her into signing over the trust deed to the Double H to him.

No, wait a minute now, she told herself. Then you were young and totally naïve.

Last night you weren't.

Mark was still a bastard.

But, looking over at Jake, she was forced to admit he didn't qualify for that distinction. In fact, what he qualified for was an apology from her. She had mocked him in front of his colleagues. She had no right to do that to him. And he hadn't done anything to deserve that from her. If her Dad had taught her anything when she was growing up, it was that when you made a mistake, it was your duty to apologize for it if you hurt someone because of that mistake.

Riley resolved to apology to Jake just as soon as she had the opportunity to speak to him privately. Till then she needed to focus on the current conversation.

"Alexei Zhukov was one of Étienne Devereux's most valuable customers," Riley told the group. "In fact, Étienne told me once that besides being Zhukov's banker here in Monaco, they were also business partners in several big international ventures."

"Do you know what ventures they were partnered on?" Jake asked her.

Riley shook her head in response. "Étienne just talked in generalities. When it actually came to business, he was always very careful not to give details."

She looked over at Jake. "At least to me, that is. I don't know how he was with other people."

"Like Bill Larson," Claudine said.

Riley could only shrug at that.

"It seems to me that Étienne being dead would create all kinds of business problems for Zhukov," she said. "Besides that, they seemed to be really good friends. I mean, he was the one Étienne asked to escort Constanza to that charity dinner the night he died.

"So what reason could he possibly have for wanting Étienne dead?"

"Riley's got a point," Max said to Jake and the others. "We know for a fact that there were more than a few people Étienne did business with who had a real reason to want him dead."

"Or thought they had a real reason," Apollo said.

"Are you checking them out?" Riley asked Jake.

"Of course," Jake said stiffly.

"What about Minister Hamidi?" she asked.

"What about him?"

"Do you think what happened could have had anything to do with him?"

"Why do you ask that?" Derrick said.

"Well," Riley with a hesitant half shrug. "He's from Afghanistan."

Derrick nodded to encourage her to continue.

"Étienne didn't say anything specifically to me," she said. "But Bill Larson mentioned one day recently that Étienne had confided in him that

Zhukov was secretly trying to negotiate a deal to run an oil pipeline through Afghanistan from his oil depots in Russia."

This grabbed everyone's attention as she continued.

"Not only was Étienne's bank going to fund the deal, but Étienne was also an equity partner in the deal."

"Hamidi is the Minister of Health and Education," Claudine said. "His department wouldn't be involved."

Riley turned towards her. "True. But maybe he was brokering the deal for them."

"That would make sense," Derrick said to Jake.

"If that's true," Max said. "Then he sure as heck wouldn't want Devereux dead."

"Of course not," Riley agreed. "But what if a political rival did?"

Jake turned to Derrick. "Or the Pakis did."

"Pakistan?" Riley said. "Why Pakistan? It wouldn't affect them."

"Yes it would." Jake told her. "They're pumping Russian oil down to Karachi."

"But is it Zhukov's oil? Or one of his rivals?" Apollo asked.

"Good question." Jake said.

CHAPTER 25

Apollo turned and started back to his laptop. "I'll check it out."

Jake looked over at Derrick. "I'll see what I can dig up on Hamidi," Derrick said as he followed Apollo across the room.

"Claudine," Jake said "Find out where Moreau is on Gabrielle's case."

"Where are we on tracking down the sniper's launch tube?" Jake asked Max.

"Nowhere so far." Max answered. "Kabul insisted that they never inventoried any of the Russian left behinds."

"Bull," Jake said. "The Taliban was selling that crap to any arms dealer with a suitcase full of money. There's an inventory somewhere. Find it."

Max didn't exactly look hopeful when he nodded at Jake and headed for his own laptop.

Finally alone with Jake, Riley waited until Max was out of earshot and Claudine was totally focused on the data flowing across her monitor. Jake was just turning to walk away from her when she said, "Can we talk?"

Pausing, he gave her a blank stare and a clipped nod.

Nervously licking her dry lips in order to moisten them, Riley took a deep breath and said. "I owe you an apology. I was out of line before."

Jake stood silently regarding her for several long heartbeats. "All right," he said and once again turned to leave.

"Wait," Riley called out to him.

And once again he turned to look at her.

"About last night," she stumbled in embarrassment. "It was. . . ."

"Nothing," Jake cut her off brusquely.

"Nothing!" Riley's eyes widened as she blanched in disbelief.

"Now if you'll excuse me," Jake said coldly, "I've got work to do."

Although everyone around them appeared to be busy with their individual tasks, Riley had the uncanny feeling they were listening to every word between her and Jake. Throwing a quick nervous glance around her, Riley then turned back to Jake who now stood there with his right arm crossed so that he could grip his injured left arm.

"Is there anything I can do to help?" she asked him.

"No," he said abruptly.

"How's your arm?" she asked trying to ease the awkwardness of the situation.

"It's fine, thank you."

Riley looked around the salon at the team members focused on their various monitors.

Turning back to Jake she asked. "Would it be OK if I just watched?"

"I think that you'd probably be more comfortable down in your suite. You'd have more room down there," he said.

Riley stared at him in silence. She didn't know whether to be mortified or mad. She had said she was sorry. What else was she supposed to do? Grovel?

What was he mad about? She had apologized to him. What more did he want?

And besides that, what right did he have to be mad? Last night was probably the best sex he had ever had too. So he should be thanking her, instead of her apologizing to him.

In fact, the more she thought about it, the more she realized that she was the one who should be mad, if either one of them was going to be angry about something.

The least he could have done was wake her up to tell her he was leaving. But he didn't do that. He snuck out on her while she was still sleeping. She glared at him. He didn't 'date call girls' indeed. Of course he didn't when there were women around as stupid as she had been last night.

"Right," she said to him. "The suite."

As she turned to stomp out, she paused long enough to say, "Please don't come knocking."

That finally got a response out of Jake. He cocked an eyebrow at her as she added, "Call. Or send somebody else to fetch me."

With that Riley stalked out of the room as Jake's companions stopped all pretense of being occupied so they could follow her exit.

The second Claudine heard the elevator door close behind Riley she turned to stare at Jake.

"I cannot believe that you just did that to her!"

"What?" he said genuinely confused. "I didn't say anything?"

Derrick, Apollo and Max kept a united front of male silence as they waited to see how Jake fared against Nature's deadliest weapon – a woman's outrage.

With a sneer of contempt that only a Frenchman – or in this case, Frenchwoman – can produce, Claudine tossed aside his puny excuse like it was a used tissue. "You didn't do anything?" she said with fire sparking in her eyes.

Shaking her head at him in disbelief she continued. "That poor woman apologized to you. And you sent her away to her room like she's a naughty child."

Claudine looked over at her silent teammates and shook her head in disbelief. "*Mon Dieu*," she said throwing up her hands in supplication. "Can you believe him?"

"Whoa," Max said. "Don't get us into this."

As soon as the words were out of his mouth and hit her ear, Max knew he'd made a major mistake. Throwing up his hands as if to stop a charging bull, Max told Claudine – and Jake, "We're just over here working and minding our own business."

Claudine glared at him akimbo. "Are you telling me that you don't like Riley."

"Hey, he never said that," Apollo protested.

Glad for Apollo's support, Max answered back. "Yah, I never said that. I like her fine. She's pretty feisty for a civilian."

Claudine rolled her eyes at him and then turned back to Jake - who's been watching her with a smile ghosting his lips – and lasered in on him.

Talk about feisty Jake thought to himself. You can always depend upon the French for a good show when it came to emotional displays.

Entertaining for sure. But not particularly useful when you've got a killer on the loose like now.

"Claudine, look around," he said indicating the piles of their equipment filling the salon. "There's really nowhere here for Riley to be comfortable. At least downstairs she can relax and until we have something to tell her."

Claudine just shook her head at him. "To quote a wise Frenchman," she told him. "A chair, is a chair, is a chair."

Across the room Apollo leaned towards Derrick and whispered, "I thought it was something about a rose."

Jake turned to Derrick as well. "Was I out of line?"

Derrick surprised him when he said in reply, "Maybe a tad."

"There, you heard him," Claudine said triumphantly to Jake. "Now go below and apologize to the woman."

Shaking his head at Claudine, Jake looked over at Derrick for guidance.

"It wouldn't hurt," Derrick said.

Indicating Claudine who still had her fisted hands on her hips in indignation, Derrick continued. "And we could all get back to work."

Sighing like a martyr, Jake gave up the fight. "All right," he told Claudine. "I'll go apologize to her."

Shaking his head at what he had to put up with from his teammates, Jake headed for the lobby elevator. As he did, Claudine called after him. "Make sure you bring her back with you."

~~~

Jake's knock brought Riley to the suite's double doors. Opening the right panel just wide enough to see who it was, Riley waited for him to speak. Although her eyes were dry, her face was drawn and pale as she regarded him silently.

"May I come in?" he asked.

"No," she said. "I don't think that's a good idea."

Jake wanted to tell her of course it wasn't a good idea. Not if he was going to protect her by not letting into his life.

Instead he said, "We need to talk."

Riley was too tired to talk. She wanted to tell of him of course they needed to talk. They needed to understand if what they shared the night before was worth fighting to stay together for.

Instead she said, "There's nothing for either of us to say."

Jake looked at her. "That's not true. I owe you an explanation."

"No," Riley said briefly closing her eyes to him. "You don't owe me anything. What happened between us last night was just biology."

"Biology?" Jake said stepping closer to her. "That was a lot more than 'biology'."

Riley gave him a sad smile. "No, Jake. What happened last night was just our way of coping with being ambushed and almost dying."

"Twice," Jake reminded her trying to trigger at least a spark of a smile from her.

Sensing what he wanted from her, Riley offered him the faintest ghost of a smile as she said, "Yes, twice."

Jake relaxed slightly. If he can get a smile out of her, he can get her to agree to talk to him so he can explain why the best thing for her to do was to walk away from him while she's still safe. Or, at least she will be once they nail Étienne Devereux's killer.

Seeing the tension start to drain out of his shoulders, Riley acted to spare them both further grief.

Pulling her spine straight so that she look far more assured that she truly was, Riley lifted her chin and said, "We're just two adults who enjoy sex. That's all we are.

"And that's all last night was about? Just an enjoyable evening of casual sex between two consenting adults?"

She looked him straight in the eye. "That's all it was, Jake. Let's not try and pretend it was anything more than what it was. Casual sex."

She saw his jaw tighten as she stepped back into the room, "Now if you don't mind."

"Please go away," she said then closed the door between.

~~~

Jake stared at the closed door in silence while he tried to determine what the turmoil of emotions he was experiencing were.

Relief?

Disappointment?

Sadness?

Regret?

Loss?

He really didn't know.

All he did know for sure was that Riley was going to be safe now that he had convinced her to walk away from him.

Turning, he started back down the silent corridor towards the waiting elevator. Claudine was going to try to give him grief when he showed up without Riley at his side like she was expecting. But he'd just explain to her that Riley was resting and would join them later when she felt up to it.

He got halfway down the corridor when it hit.

Anger.

What the bloody hell was the matter with him?

Whipping back around he stalked back to the suite and pounded his fist on the door. "Riley, open the door!"

For a moment there was only the sound of his hard breathing filling his ears. Then he heard the faintest rustle of clothing as Riley approached the door.

Taking a step back from the door as she swung it open, Jake confronted her with eyes blazing.

"I don't do casual," he announced as he stepped towards her. Before she could retreat even a step he grabbed her and kissed her as if his life depended upon it.

At first she was as rigid as stone in his arms. Her lips chilled and locked tight against his flaming tongue. Pinning her tight against the door panel behind her, he pressed the length of his body against her curves. Slowly, but steadily his heat engulfed her and she began to melt into his arms as her mouth opened to let him in.

"This isn't right," she moaned as his heat engulfed her.

"I don't care if it's right or wrong," Jake whispered to her. "I've got to have you," he groaned sweeping her up into his arms.

"Now," he said as he kicked the door closed behind them and carried her up the stairs to their waiting bed.

CHAPTER 26

The sun was low in the afternoon sky when Jake finally returned with Riley at his side as instructed. Entering the salon they found it empty. The only sound that greeted them was the soft hum of the electronic gear filling the room.

A distant laugh sent them weaning their way to the rear of the salon and through its open glass doors to the sun-filled rear sun deck. An oversized chrome and black barbeque grill was loaded with sizzling steaks as Derrick played steak wrangler for his companions. And speaking of his companions, Jake took in the sight of them casually lounging in an assortment of deck chairs with chilled drinks in their hands.

"Well it's about time you two finally showed up," Apollo called out when he spotted them.

"Yeah, if you were any later you were going to have to make the next beer run," Max added as he laughingly hailed them with his half empty bottle of beer.

Turning around to peer at them through the rising clouds of smoke billowing out of the grill, Derricked called out to them. "How do you like your meat cooked?"

Laughing and shaking his head at them Jake guided Riley to the empty deck chair next to Claudine. Leaning next to her cheek he asked, "Would you like a beer?"

"That would be wonderful," she smiled at him.

As he went to collect their drinks, Claudine looked Riley straight in the eye. "Are you two OK now?"

Blushing happily Riley grinned at her. "We're fine."

Nodding contentedly, Claudine settled back in her chair and turned her face to the sun.

"Thank you," Riley whispered to her. "Jake told me what you did."

Never turning her face away from the sunlight pouring down on her, Claudine said, "If you want it done right, sometimes it takes a woman to do a man's job."

Riley was still chuckling when Jake returned with their cold beers. Just as he handed one to her Derrick called over to them.

"Jake, Riley – have you two got a minute?"

"Sure," Jake answered as Riley got up and together they crossed over to the grill to stand upwind of the fire.

"What's up?" Jake asked as Derrick worked his way through a line of steaks, turning them one by one.

"While you two were otherwise engaged," Derrick said with a hint of a twinkle in his eye. "The rest of us were slaving away over our hot keyboards."

"And what did you find while you were slaving away?" Jake joked back at him.

The light banter disappeared from Derrick's tone as he looked over at Jake and Riley. "We did some real deep digging on Zhukov and his dealings with Étienne Devereux."

"What about Hamidi?" Riley asked.

"Him too," Derrick assured her.

"What did you find?" Jake said.

"Some really interesting information," Apollo answered as he, Max and Claudine joined their group.

"Hamidi's brother is the Minister of the Interior," Derrick said. "The Ministry of Mines is under him."

"Afghanistan's mineral wealth is currently estimated to be in the billions," Apollo added.

"And that number is increasing almost daily as more and more surveys are uncovering still more undiscovered sites," Derrick told them.

"But the country currently has no infrastructure in place to allow for the transportation of anything that does get mined," Max said.

"Okay," Jake said. "Where are we going with this?"

"China, Iran and North Korea are the leading contenders for mining rights," Derrick explained.

He turned to Riley. "You were right. Étienne Devereux was just more that Zhukov's banker. They were also business partners, just like Étienne told you."

Derrick looked over at Jake as he continued, "The two of them were planning on locking up all of the construction projects in the country – both mining and all of the transportation systems."

"That's a smart move," Riley said. "If you can't get your product to the marketplace, you can't sell it. If they control the roads giving access to the mines and the marketplaces, they're in the position to control the entire country."

"And its wealth," Claudine said.

Derrick and Jake nodded in agreement with her assessment.

"China and the others might have a lock on the actual mining operation rights," Max said. "But Devereux had pulled together a consortium of investors to fund the massive construction projects."

"And that also included two major oil pipelines," Claudine said. "They would run both north/south and east/west through the country."

"Does Islamabad know about this?" Jake asked Derrick.

Derrick shook his head in reply. "Not as far as we could find out."

"What happens to the deal now that Étienne Devereux is dead?" Riley said. "Is it still going to go forward?"

Jake looked at her. "I can't imagine that it won't. We're talking about a multi-billion dollar series of construction projects," he said.

"The question is who controls it now?" Claudine said.

"With Devereux dead that just leaves Alexei Zhukov running the show," Apollo said.

Derrick locked eyes with Jake and Riley. "Sounds like we may have just figured out why the robbers didn't grab Devereux for the ransom. He was more valuable dead than alive."

"But Zhukov doesn't control the project," Riley said.

"What do you mean?" Jake asked her.

"The bank actually controls the project since its funding it," Riley said.

She looked around at the others and then continued. "Constanza is Étienne's sole heir. She controls the bank now."

Riley turned to Jake. "That means she controls the project. Not Zhukov."

"The question is, does Alexei Zhukov know," Claudine said.

"Of course he knows," Jake told her.

"If Alexei Zhukov is responsible for Étienne's death," Riley said. "That means that Constanza is in danger."

"So what are we going to do?" Apollo said. "We don't actually have any proof to take to Moreau."

He looked over at Riley as he continued. "Or to Constanza."

Jake grinned at Apollo. "There's only one thing we can do."

"What?" Riley asked him.

He gave her a smile as cold as a crocodile's as he said, "Get him to confess."

"And get it on tape," Apollo, Max and Claudine said in unison.

Riley looked back and forth between Jake and the others and then let out a laugh. "I gather you've done this before?" she said.

This time Jake's smile for her was genuine. "A time or two."

CHAPTER 27

"I never should have listened to you," Jake said as they approached the ornate open gates to Constanza Devereux's Cap-Ferrat mansion. "It's too dangerous,"

"Give it up, Rafferty," Riley said. "I'm going in you with. Whether you like it or not."

Jake shook his head at her as he entered the serpentine driveway that led up to the main house.

"I'm the one he tried to have killed three times," she reminded him. "I earned the right to be there when you pull the rug out from under him."

As the sweeping lines of the apricot colored mansion came into view around the last bend in the driveway, Riley grinned over at Jake. "Besides that you need me in there since I'm the one wearing the wire."

"I could have worn it," he said as he pulled up in front of the house with its apron of low steps.

"You don't have the right curves," she cheerfully told him as she opened her door and climbed out of the SUV.

Rounding the front of the car to join him at the base of the front steps she grinned at him as they hurried up the broad low steps towards the liveried butler standing in the open doorway.

"I'm glad that you didn't bring the Ferrari," she whispered to him as they moved up the steps.

"Why?"

"The red would have clashed terribly with the color of the house."

~~~

"Jake," Constanza smiled at him from the divan in front of the fireplace as he and Riley entered the drafty drawing room.

"Nurse Copper," she continued with a frosty glance at Riley. "Alexei told me you were out on bail."

Both Jake and Riley looked over at Alexei Zhukov who had been using an iron poker to stir the burning logs in the fireplace. Returning the poker to its holder on the stone hearth he turned towards them. Casually slipping his left hand into the pocket of his evening jacket, he gave them a nod of greeting. Riley watched as he remained standing by the fire with the wall at his back.

"Miss Copper is no longer a suspect in Étienne's death," Jake told Constanza as he locked eyes with the Russian.

"Oh, really? Do the police know who stole my necklace?"

"Not yet," Riley answered for Jake. "But they should be picking him up soon."

"Him?" Constanza said to Jake as if Riley wasn't even in the room.

"And Constanza's necklace?" Zhukov spoke for the first time. "Has it been recovered yet?"

Riley had always been surprised that he spoke with the faintest of a British accent. Then Étienne had explained to her that Zhukov's father had been a diplomat at the Russian Embassy in London for many years. And that his good friend Alexei had actually graduated from Cambridge.

"No," Jake said.

"How disappointing," Zhukov commented.

"Not as disappointing as finding out that you killed Étienne," Jake retorted.

"Me?" Zhukov shook his head and laughed. "Don't be ridiculous. I was at the Palace with Constanza when the fire broke out."

"You should know that," Constanza said sharply. "Your people were with us the entire evening."

As Constanza glared at her and Jake, Riley ignored her and addressed Alexei. "We know about Gabrielle and Bill Larson?"

"Who is Gabrielle?" Constanza demanded to know.

"Gabrielle LeFleuer," Riley said. She returned her gaze to Zhukov. "Or do you prefer Olga Smalyaninova?"

"I've never heard of the woman," Constanza said. "Who is she and what does she have with anything?

"She worked for Alexei as a spy," Riley told her.

Constanza laughed. "Spy? That's really melodramatic, don't you think?

Riley gave her a hard look. "Would you prefer 'call girl'? Or even 'prostitute' instead?"

Never taking his eyes off of Zhukov, Jake asked Constanza, "Were you aware that Étienne and Alexei here were partners in a deal to build an oil pipeline in Afghanistan?"

Constanza dismissively waved her hand at him. "Of course I was. Étienne and I discussed everything."

Giving Jake an icy look she continued, "Our bank is funding the project."

She threw a glance over at Riley as she said, "And for your information the deal is still going forward."

Getting up off of the couch, Constanza crossed over to Zhukov's side to show her solidarity with him. "I can't imagine why you thought that I'd believe a word of this dribble for a single moment."

Suddenly Constanza's eyes darted between Jake and Riley. Then a smug smile filled her face.

'Of course," she said to Jake. "You're sleeping with her, aren't you?"

Laughing at the two of them, she shook her head in amusement. "You think this is going to keep her from going to prison, don't you?"

"Really, Jake. With all of the women in Monaco who would be more than delighted to share your bed," she said. "I really would have thought that you could do better than this."

Catching a glimpse of Jake out of the corner of her eye, Riley followed his lead and didn't react to Constanza's insult.

Constanza turned to Zhukov and said, "That explains why they're trying to blame you for what happened."

Constanza turned back towards Jake. "You're no longer welcome in my house." She waved a bejeweled hand in Riley's direction. "Take her and go."

Zhukov used the distraction of Constanza to make his move.

Anticipating him, Jake's gun was just clearing his holster when Zhukov's sniper fired through the drawing room window. Since he was standing sideways to the window, the round caught Jake in his bad shoulder and slammed him against the stone of the fireplace, then ricocheted him to the floor. The force of the body blow sent his gun flying out of his hand and skidding across the floor to land near Riley.

As she started to dive for it, Zhukov hooked a startled Constanza around the neck with his left arm. At the same time, he pulled his gun out of his right pocket and pressed the tip of the barrel against her right temple.

"Touch it and you both die," Zhukov said in a voice that left no doubt he would do just that.

"Okay," Riley said as she straightened up and held her hands away from her body at hip level.

"Back away from it," he commanded as he tightened his hold on Constanza's neck.

Wrapping her hands around his forearm, Constanza struggled to break his hold enough so she could breathe. As Zhukov tightened his grip on her neck Constanza locked her eyes on Riley's face.

Something about the determination – and fury in her eyes – got through to Riley.

"Jake, are you OK?" Riley called out to him as she kept her eyes locked on Zhukov and Constanza.

As Jake gave a muffled grunt in response, Riley saw Constanza take her left hand off of Zhukov's forearm and drop it next to her side – just inches from the fireplace set with its iron poker.

"Alexei, you didn't really think that we'd walk in here alone? Did you?" Riley asked.

Before he could reply, Constanza wrapped her hand around the iron poker. In the blink of an eye she had it out and arcing down across Zhukov's gun hand.

Years on the tennis court drove her swing with the force of a pile driver. Both Jake and Riley heard Zhukov's wrist bone snap as the gun when flying out of his hand.

From his vantage point sprawled on the floor Jake watched as Riley leapt forward and caught the gun in mid air. She had it centered on Zhukov's forehead with the same speed that Constanza had delivered her crippling blow.

"Please give me an excuse to blow your brains out," she growled at him in a guttural voice.

Never taking her eyes off of Zhukov hunched over against the fire place, cradling his injured wrist, Riley called over her shoulder to Constanza. "Are you all right?"

Spent and shaken the older woman slumped on the edge of the divan near when Jake's gun had landed.

"Yes," she answered shakily.

Looking across the room at Jake, she asked, "He did it, didn't he? He killed Étienne?"

"I'm sorry," Jake told her.

From the front of the house all of them heard the crash of the front door exploding open.

"What . . . ?" Constanza cried out in a startled voice.

With her eyes still locked on Zhukov's, Riley announced brightly, "Sounds like the cavalry has finally arrived."

As Zhukov drew himself upright to stare contemptuously at her, Riley barely had time to register the soft swish of silk when a shot rang out next to her right ear. At the same instance, a third eye blossomed in the middle of Zhukov's forehead.

CAROL A. HUGHES

CHAPTER 28

Riley watched Paris slide past her train window as the Marseilles-Paris Express pulled into the *Gare du Nord* station. She had always been in love with Paris. It was a city of and for romantics. Love was its life blood.

She had always seen it as a city pulsating with life, love, and *joie de vie*

Until today.

Pull yourself together Copper, she scolded herself as she gathered up her purse and shoulder bag. You've got $15 million sitting in the bank and you're on your way to teach Mark Scanlon what happens when he messes with the wrong cowgirl.

She could thank Constanza Devereux for the $15 million.

Not that the woman ever intended for her to earn a penny more than her nurse's salary. But Constanza hadn't counted on Riley's sudden stroke of insight that allowed her to figure out the truth about the allegedly missing necklace that was the key to unraveling the mystery behind Étienne Devereux's death.

If the robbery was merely staged to camouflage the real objective of the attack on the penthouse, Riley reasoned to Jake.

"Then what if the theft of the necklace was also a camouflage?" she had asked.

Well it turned out she was more right than anyone expected.

As head of Étienne's security, Jake knew the combination to all of Devereux's safes. So opening the one at the mansion was no problem.

And finding the necklace in its purple velvet bag was definitely the icing on the cake.

Constanza really believed that not only was she going to collect the full $157 million the insurance company was preparing to pay out on the loss of her eponymous necklace. But secretly keep the necklace, which had been in the safe of her Cap-Ferrat mansion the whole time, as well.

Luckily for her, Riley thought, the insurance company was happier to pay her the $15 million in finder's fees, than hand over the full $157 million to Constanza for a necklace that had never been stolen in the first place.

She should dislike the woman just on general principles alone. But her saving grace had been the fact that, despite all of her faults, she had truly loved her husband.

OK, that and the fact that she had helped save their lives.

Jake was having a hard time over the fact that Constanza wasn't going to be charged with anything since she had withdrawn her insurance claim. And her battery of lawyers had insisted that their "poor client" had been so distraught by her husband's tragic death, that she hadn't remembered him leaving the real necklace in the mansion's safe.

As for her shooting Alexei Zhukov – her publicist had turned her into a modern day Joan of Arc. She was France's own tragic heroine. The public and the media loved her. And there wasn't a prosecutor in the entire country willing to chance bringing their wraith down on them by filing a single charge against her.

Riley had to admit that, while Constanza definitely was someone she really did not want to get to know better. At least she had an interesting way of looking at life when she offered up her tidbit of advice upon the discovery of the necklace in her own safe.

"A woman can never be too thin, have too much money, or too many diamonds." she sagely told Jake

And speaking of money – Constanza was now going to be rolling in it. With Zhukov permanently out of the picture, and her now in control of Étienne's bank, that left her as the sole partner in the planned Afghanistan venture.

Some women seemed to have all of the luck in the world. Whether they deserved it or not, Riley thought despondently as she trudged down the side corridor of her train car, following the line of passengers ahead of her out of the car and onto the platform.

She thought that she was one of them when Jake had convinced the insurance company that she had earned their finder's fee. The money was nice, she didn't want anyone to think that she didn't appreciate it.

But the month she and Jake spent together, while he was recovering from being shot, had been beyond incredible. And then overnight he suddenly started pulling back from her.

She didn't need to be a genius to figure out what was going on between them. A living rival she might have been able to overcome. But, pardon the pun, she though – she didn't stand a 'ghost' of a chance against the two ghosts who owned Jake's heart.

So here she was in Paris about to catch her connecting train to London and the flight home to face her own ghosts. The only problem was that in her haste to get away from the pain of her defeat – she had left her heart in Monaco.

Since the porters were handling the transfer of her luggage over to the London bound bullet train she had 15 minutes to spare before she was due to board the new train. Glancing around at the grand old Victorian station, Riley heard herself let out a sigh.

"That doesn't sound like someone who's happy to see Paris," a familiar voice said from behind her.

Spinning around she was startled to find Jake standing there grinning at her.

"What are you doing here?"

"Collecting your luggage," he said as he jerked his thumb over his shoulder at the porter who was pulling her bags off of the bullet train trolley and loading them onto a separate trolley.

"What are you doing with my luggage," she said. "I'm going to miss my connection."

"What do you think about a honeymoon in Paris?" Jake said instead of answering her question.

"Honeymoon? Whose?"

"Ours, of course. After all, Paris is the city of love."

"It is?"

"Of course." he said grinning at her. "At least that's what I've been told."

"You have?"

He nodded at her. "Haven't you?"

Slowly she nodded back.

"So will you?"

"Will I what?"

"Marry me."

"Marry . . ?"

Riley looked around at the crowd of travelers swirling around them.

"And after the honeymoon," Jake said gently grabbing her chin and turning her gaze back to him. "What do you say about you and me taking a little trip to Wyoming and teaching that ex of yours a lesson about stealing from my wife."

"Your wife?"

Jake nodded as he leaned in and gently brushed his lips across hers. "That's what I said." The tip of his tongue flicked out and softly parted her lips.

"Now what do you say?" he murmured as softly as a summer breeze skipping through sunlit leaves.

"Yes," she sighed melting completely into his warm embrace.

CAROL A. HUGHES

Paris

City of Light - City of Dark

City of Love - City of Death

In the dark nobody knows her name. In the dark nobody hears her scream.

In Paris one man wants her dead. In Paris one man wants her love.

Both will kill to ensure it.

Will Zoe Bennett survive the Danger in Paris?

COMING OCTOBER 2013

The second book in this exciting series.

ABOUT THE AUTHOR

In another time, and another life, author Carol A. Hughes walked the same dark streets and alleyways found here in the *DANGER* series.

www.ingramcontent.com/pod-product-compliance
Lightning Source LLC
Chambersburg PA
CBHW071713140626
46557CB00011B/47